The "It" Girls

of

La Sembradora

Bulls, Blood and

Brujería

Nancy de la Zerda

This story is a work of fiction. Names, characters, places
and events are the product of the author's imagination.
Any resemblance to actual persons, living or dead,
business establishments or locales is entirely
coincidental.

The "It" Girls

of

La Sembradora

Bulls, Blood and Brujería

Nancy de la Zerda

Acknowledgments

A special thanks to all my writers-in-arms who helped edit and shape this story: Jim Goodgion's group at the Northeast Senior Center and Jack Ward's group at Barnes and Noble in San Antonio. Most especially, a nod to Christina Smith, who helped immensely in getting this *novela* started.

Thanks to my family for encouraging me to write and giving me ever-present support. To my sisters, Olga, Olivia and Becky, for providing much fodder for the characters' banter in this story. A wistful thanks to Norma Jasmer-DeSimone, who shared many of my "coming of age" adventures.

Motivation to publish this story was provided by my brother, Alfred De La Zerda, "The Doctor", who recently published his first novel, "Acapulco." Also, thanks to my cousin, Norma Alarcón, whose love of literature inspires everyone around her.

Thanks to Mom for weaving tales and Dad for believing in the power of education.

To my mom,

Olga Cantú de la Zerda

A true "it" girl
And constant inspiration.

n.z.

"Thou hast nor youth nor age;
But, as it were, an after-dinner's sleep,
Dreaming on both."

William Shakespeare

The "It" Girls

of

La Sembradora

Bulls, Blood and Brujería

Nancy de la Zerda

6

Prologue

My cousin Eva and I couldn't help it if other girls in La Sembradora avoided us. They admired Eva well enough, but preferred to do so from a distance, especially in the presence of their boyfriends or admirers. Eva's exotic appearance and lively charm seemed to eclipse everyone else's. She mesmerized others unwittingly, which made her all the more a source of envy for the girls.

I got tiny waves and polite nods as they hurried away. Many of them owed me money for anything from candy to silk stockings and perfumes I peddled for Mamá. She'd converted our parlor into a tiny general store when Papá was killed in an accident years earlier. I helped by selling goods from the store at school and in our neighborhood. When I began to extend credit, my business doubled, but my social circle shrank. Though I never attempted to collect money in social settings, my presence was enough to jar some of the girls and remind them they still owed for the very stockings they wore or the fragrances they reeked of.

They invariably smiled as they departed, eager to stay in my good graces, since such commodities were hard to come by in dusty 1930's La Sembradora, a tiny village in northern Mexico. I accompanied Mamá on monthly excursions by train to the border, where she purchased ladies' lingerie and toiletries on "the other side" in Eagle Pass, Texas. Most purchases were based on orders. I sold any extras Mamá could afford. For most of my customers, I was the only source for such coveted goods.

It was a great time for coming of age in La Sembradora. Despite unpaved roads, the village was busy with traffic. Pedestrians gripped black parasols and hurried along the shade of adobe houses and cement block buildings. Vendors ambled down the middle of the road, in full sun, balancing huge baskets atop their heads and barking tempting slogans about their wares. Others pushed carts down the road to the main plaza, where they hawked everything from fresh pineapple slices and roasted corn to huaraches and sewing needles. Old men sat on plaza benches nodding their sombreros, exchanging stories. Young men huddled boisterously at cafés, poking fun at each other and anyone who strolled by. Servants hurried along, toting bags filled with fresh fruits and vegetables from the market for their employers' noon meals.

A rusty bus lumbered along the well-worn main road carrying commuters to jobs, village shops or to a bus station in the neighboring town, La Cosecha. On its return, the bus carried a capacity-load of travelers from other parts of the region to La Sembradora's train station, the only one in the area.

Most travel outside the region was by train, since paved roads were scant and very few people owned automobiles. This ensured La Sembradora an economic boost and a livelier social ambiance than might be expected for a dusty village in arid northern Mexico. The neighboring town, La Cosecha, more prosperous and industrial than ours, boasted a steel mill that provided further opportunities for business and pleasure.

La Sembradora's only movie theatre was an enclosed building with no roof. We happily sat on splintered benches to marvel at Hollywood films and squint to study the Spanish captions while actors like Rudolph Valentino, Charlie Chaplin and Clara Bow, the "it girl" of film, entertained us. We sighed as we watched them move about the "screen", a set of worn, whitewashed boards that doubled as the theatre's front wall.

We lived in a village too remote to attract many celebrities. But La Sembradora, yet missing on many maps, boasted the biggest bullring in the region. Famous matadors drew the largest crowds and stirred much excitement throughout the area. Eva and I were a bit squeamish about some scenes at the bullfights. Yet, the music, the sights and sounds of the bustling arena crowds in the stands, as well as the great pomp and circumstance of rituals performed in the bullring, more than made up for our having to turn away at times once the bull entered.

We watched enthralled from the opening scenes when *picadores* bounced about the arena on horseback and *banderilleros* marched around the bullring holding colorfully decorated wooden spears. We were riveted at the sight of the matadors, each dressed in a distinctive, sequined "suit of lights", swirling colorful capes as they strutted about the sandy bullring waving at the crowds.

But what Eva and I relished most was dressing up for such occasions. We took great care in every detail so that we emerged quite ready, not only to turn heads, but also, to have the best possible times of our young lives.

Tardeadas, special afternoon socials, were held at the private casino in La Cosecha after each bullfight. The casino was a place where many socials took place, from ladies' canasta games to private weddings. Only members and their guests could attend. Sunday afternoon *tardeadas* were the most coveted social events in the region. Few girls from our village ever attended.

But Eva and I were especially fortunate and set apart from them in another way. Though we attended all socials chaperoned, as was the custom, Mamá and Eva's parents were honored when a family friend, the elegant Federico (or Rico as everyone called him), a perpetual bachelor and man-about-town, adopted us as his young charges. He became our constant escort and lifelong friend. Everyone ignored his *volteado* touches like makeup and tweezed brows, not because they approved of *"la vida alegre"*, but because his family was very wealthy by La Sembradora standards. His mother and father were godparents to many children in the village, including Eva and me. He was a member of the casino in La Cosecha and his social calendar was peppered with invitations to many exclusive events that we would otherwise have missed. Consequently, Eva and I attended socials other girls our age only wondered about. And what girlish fun we had!

Mamá made our dresses from bolts of fabric she sold. Eva and I studied the latest hairdos in magazines and those worn by the most beautiful actresses in the movies. We styled each other's hair. When we dressed up, we appeared much older than we were. Perfume, makeup and high heels transformed much more than our appearances. They thrust us into a palpable Cinderella-at-the-ball magic where we escaped the mundane reality of La Sembradora and became enchantresses, if only for a few hours. Rico often commented, "You two don't enter a room. You arrive!"

My cousin Eva bewitched even the worldliest matadors at Sunday *tardeadas*. Bullfighters at the bar celebrating their afternoon heroics faltered when she walked in. Their hearty laughter and back slaps froze mid-air. Chatter throughout the casino died. Heads turned in her direction.

She clicked her charm across the room in satin heels. Her soft curves and svelte figure were always showcased in the latest European design. A saucy hat atop her dark, perfectly coiffed hair set her apart. High cheekbones, Dolores del Río eyes, full red lips and smooth olive skin secured Eva an exotic mystique. Her commanding poise and startling glamour arrested eyes while her infectious playfulness captivated hearts. Even the dourest old lady surrendered a smile when caught in the mirror of Eva's eyes.

A bit shorter and much paler than my beautiful cousin, I'd wobble in my high heels alongside her, self-conscious, wary that too much attention would render us a case of the evil eye. Alone, my looks and style might turn a few heads, but at Eva's side, it was as if I'd been thrust onto a light-flooded stage. I shied awkward in the palpable energy of so many stares. As I walked, others in the room seemed to blur, a distant audience, as I focused on our destination, all the while smiling and chatting with my companions.

On those dreamy nights, Rico linked arms with Eva and me, paraded us across dance floors, secured best tables, glared commands. Bevies of waiters scrambled about, pulled squeaky chairs, snapped fresh tablecloths in place and filled crystal goblets of La

Contesa cognac for Rico, mineral water for us girls. Friends and neighbors gathered round, paid homage to Rico, got close-up looks of his young charges and always asked us about our dresses.

Big band sounds *á la mexicana* wove romance those nights. Seasoned partners smoothed around the dance floor, while others stubbed toes in jagged attempts at connection. Between melodies, dancers buzzed in festive swarms of youthful flirtation and gawky lust. While Eva held court, all giggle-wink, I bantered with the boys. Rico drank in every move…and a lot of La Contesa.

He danced only with Eva and me to claim his place in the whirlwind of our entourage. At each *tardeada*, at least one intrepid matador fought his way toward Eva, only to be tossed a smile-blink-shrug from her as Rico graced her away in great ceremony. Decorum called for our polite decline of any stranger's attention. Eva and I rarely broke that rule.

Rico refused invitations that didn't include us. So we basked in our youth like unruly royalty, giggling and chortling our way through social events in the finest parlors, restaurants and casinos. If there was resentment or gossip about Rico's favoritism, we never heard it. At his side, we were untouchable. As long as our social calendars were full and Mamá pedaled away at her Singer sewing machine, we lived ecstatic.

Details of those long ago events linger vividly when I whiff an old handkerchief, gaze into yellowed photographs, touch satin to my wrinkled skin, and, most especially, when I hear the music we enjoyed. I treasure these great memories—mine to relive, savor and share with others.

Chapter One: Front Page News

"¡Inma!...¡Inma!...¡María Inmaculada! Where are you, *hija*?" Mamá called from her little store in the front part of our home.

"Coming!" I yelled.

Mamá grinned as I entered the room, which had been the parlor before Papá died. He'd been killed in a tragic accident seven years earlier, in1930. When the banks failed shortly after his untimely death, Mamá opened the tiny general store to help support her four young children. She referred to it as "*el comercio*", a big name for the tiny space that served as the hub of our universe in many ways.

"I need your help." Mamá pointed her chin toward some canned goods on the counter.

"*Ay, por favor*, I'm supposed to go out with Eva," I whined.

"There'll be plenty of time for that later. Look at all this merchandise, Inma!" She waved her arms. I noticed a huge burlap sack and several crates on the floor beside her.

"I'll get dusty, Mamá," I said. "Where is everyone?"

"*Hija*, I don't want to hear another word. If you must know, your brother has gone to make deliveries and your sisters are busy embroidering pillowcases. I've nearly sold out. Can I count on you or not?"

"*Bueno*, whatever you say." I brushed back my hair and reached into a crate.

"*Ay, qué bueno.* You know what to do with all this. I need to help Juana in the kitchen, so I'll be on my way."

"You mean I have to do all this by myself?" I frowned.

"*Ay*, Inma, it's not all that much once you get started. You'll see. You'll be done in time for lunch."

"I hope so. *Pero*, it's just not fair!"

"Careful, *hija*. I hear someone coming up the walk. Remember, things take longer when you pout. Don't forget to be courteous." She turned on her heel and walked out. "And smile!" she called over her shoulder.

16

"*Buenos días*, Inma."

I turned to face our neighbor, Doña Inez. Her wrinkled brown face twisted into a smile.

I reached into a crate and pulled out several sardine tins. "*Buenos días*, Doña Inez. What can I get you?" I kept my eyes on her and continued unpacking the crate.

"Ah, your mother has left you in charge, I see. I trust she's well."

"*Sí*, Doña, *gracias*, she's fine, only she's busy in the kitchen." I turned away from the gnarled woman to stack some canned goods on shelves behind the counter, organizing the cans according to their contents. "How can I help you?" I asked, turning my head enough to look at her as I set merchandise in place.

"*Ah, pues*, I need two aspirins. My husband's snoring has given me another headache. I tell you, he's loud as a train." She began to cackle.

I reached for the aspirin bottle Mamá kept under the counter. "Just two?" I asked.

"*Sí, pues*, that's all I can afford for now. *Gracias a Dios*, he works the night shift today, so I should be fine." She shrugged her shoulders and grinned.

"Here you go." I shook the aspirins onto a piece of brown paper, wrapped it into a tiny bundle and held it out to the old woman. "That'll be ten *centavos*."

"*Ay, gracias*." She flashed a toothless smile as she opened a tattered coin purse and sifted through the contents with her fingers. She examined several coins before handing me one.

"*Gracias*, Doña." I placed the coin in the money drawer and returned to the crates. The old woman hesitated.

"Ah, to be a young *señorita* again. I suppose you're very excited about the big bullfight coming to our little village, *¿no?*"

"What bullfight?" I stopped my chore long enough to look at her.

"*Ay, mija*, you mean you haven't read the newspaper?" She pointed at the front page of El Regional on the counter. "Isn't he the most handsome matador you've ever seen?" She studied my face.

I set two cans of peas on the counter and grabbed the newspaper. A photograph of El Victor, a popular young matador, swirling a cape over a charging bull almost filled the front page. The headlines read: "Famed Spanish Matador to Tour Mexico." I focused on the newspaper article and scanned the list of towns El Victor would tour. There it was in black and white. Our little village was included! Although it was small, La Sembradora boasted the largest bullring in northern Mexico. I blinked and read the list again. Yes, there it was! La Sembradora. "I can't believe it!" I said.

"*Ah, pero* see for yourself, it's true." The old woman sighed.

"I know. I mean, uh, it's just so wonderful. El Victor. He's my absolute favorite!"

"*Pues*, now you'll have a splendid opportunity to see him. You and your cousin Eva always go to the bullfights and *tardeadas* afterwards, *¿verdad?*"

"*Pues, sí*, most always. That is, when our friend Rico invites us."

"Surely he'll wish to attend such a grand event." The old woman gazed at me. "I suppose you may meet this young matador, what with Rico's connections."

"*Ay*, Doña, do you really think so? I might meet…El Victor?" I blinked.

"Enjoy yourselves!" The old woman smiled as she hobbled out of the store.

"*Sí, gracias, gracias.*" I nodded and stared at the photograph of the slender young matador. I was still gazing at El Victor's image minutes later when I heard a noise. I glanced toward the door and saw my cousin approaching.

"*Hola, prima.*" Eva hopped up the stairs from the walk and strolled into the store.

"Have you heard the latest?" I blurted.

"That depends. All I've heard today is that the burro is thirsty again."

"Quit trying to be funny. It's all over the newspaper. Look for yourself. El Victor is coming to La Sembradora!" I held out the front page.

She walked past me, reached into a candy jar on the counter and fished out one of the sweets. She gingerly removed the paper wrapper and popped the candy into her mouth. "You mean El Victor, the matador?"

"Who else? He's only the most famous bullfighter in the entire world!"

"He is?" She smacked as she chewed.

"That's right. El Victor, *el número uno*, that's who! He's coming here!"

"Sure, I know about it, Inma." She rolled her eyes.

"Eva, I swear, how can you just stand there? Aren't you excited?"

"Not really, since Papá told me tickets to the bullfight sold out this morning."

"Already?...*Pues*, never mind! Surely Rico managed to secure tickets. And, of course, he'll invite us to the *tardeada*. He always does. That's truly the main event, anyway. Everybody who's anybody will be there."

"I suppose so." Eva leaned against the counter and reached for another candy.

"Stop that!" I narrowed my eyes at her. "*Prima*, I don't understand you sometimes. This is the most exciting news we've had, perhaps ever, and all you can do is stand there and eat. You're exasperating!"

"*Ay tú*, Inma. I can't help it. If you must know, I ate too many *frijoles* at lunch and didn't get much of a siesta. " She studied my face as she chewed.

"Now you're just being awful. Here, help me finish stacking these." I signaled toward the crates.

Eva bared perfect teeth in a wide grin. "You know what you are, *prima*? You are no fun, that's what. A spoilsport! Not even a smile at my little joke there."

"You're impossible!" I shook my head.

"*Ay*, Inma, go on. You are excited enough for both of us about that silly matador coming to town. Besides, that's months off. Meanwhile, we're stuck here tending the store." She reached into one of the crates, placed several tins on the shelves. "I want to have some fun today!" She shrugged.

I smiled. "Of course you do, *prima. Pero* just think what fun we'll have at the *tardeada*. You'll see. This could be the biggest event of our lives!" I shoved an empty crate out of the way and reached into another.

"Is El Victor the tall *güero* one with freckles or the squatty *moreno*?" Eva wrinkled her nose.

"Look at his picture on the front page! You know perfectly well he's tall and dark, a tall *moreno*."

"No, I don't, Inma. I can't keep up with all your matadors!"

"*My* matadors? You're one to talk. Why, you're the one they fuss over at the socials. Rico has his hands full keeping them at bay."

"*Ay*, of course, dear Rico, ever the perfect chaperone."

"We are very fortunate to have him, Eva. You know that if it weren't for Rico, we would not attend half the events we do."

"I suppose. *Pero* I don't see why you go on about Rico having his hands full with me. You're the one they talk to all evening."

"Only because you get bored so easily. Not me. I like to make conversation."

"All they do is talk about themselves, Inma."

"That's not true. The matadors tell me all about bullfighting."

"You mean you listen to them boast about how *macho* they are!"

"*Ah, pero* there's much more to it than that. Bullfighting is an art. Matadors train all their lives, and the bulls..."

"*Ay, por favor*, Inma, don't go on about all that. We have much more important matters at hand, don't you think?"

"*Ah, sí*, the groceries." I reached for more tins.

"Not that. I mean our preparations for the big event."

"Such as?"

"For one thing, whatever in the world shall we wear?"

"So you *do* want to go!"

Eva quit stacking groceries, tossed back her head and laughed. As always, my cousin's mirth was

24

contagious. We were still giggling when Mamá walked in.

"*¿Qué pasa, muchachas?*" she asked.

"*Hola*, Tía." Eva smiled. "Inma and I were just wondering what to wear to a very important social."

"Sounds intriguing," Mamá said. "What social might that be?"

"Mamá, surely you read the newspaper." I waved it in the air. "El Victor, the most famous matador in all of Spain, is coming here. To La Sembradora!"

"You don't say." She grinned.

"You knew about this and didn't tell me?" I looked at my mother and waited.

"*Por supuesto.* Every customer this morning has spoken of it. *Pero* I wanted you to finish your work before you got carried away."

"*Ay*, Tía, Rico is sure to invite Inma and me to the *tardeada*," Eva said.

"That's right," I chimed. "Mamá, you'll have to make our dresses!"

"I'll be glad to, *hija*. Only let's finish putting these things away. One thing at a time." She smiled knowingly, perhaps wistfully, as she reached into a crate.

Chapter Two: Much Ado about Everything

We could never have imagined what was in store for us girls and, indeed, for everyone in the village. Never had the collective anticipation for any event reached such dramatic heights. Now, the world's most famous matador, El Victor, would travel from Madrid and tour Mexico. All La Sembradora was abuzz with excitement.

Without delay, talk of the young star's prowess grew legendary and escalated as the day of the event neared. No bull outlived an afternoon with this matador. El Victor paced, circled about doomed beasts that swirled, entranced, and followed his lead to their demise. He celebrated the very spryness of bulls. In keen, measured ritual, he orchestrated a flawless performance of man and beast in a tango of rage. Reports abounded that bulls literally promenaded into the young man's sword. Gossip purported that as El Victor delivered a singular deathblow, every man stood transfixed, many women fainted. Then the arena shook from the cheers and foot stomping. People tossed flowers onto the sand as the young matador bowed to his audience.

Embellished stories raised him to mythical altitudes among the ranks of matadors. Advertisements pictured him riding the shoulders of famous bullfighters, past and present. Ticket sales reached staggering heights. And printed word that El Victor had not yet taken a bride catapulted talk among females of all ages to the very pinnacle of the hubbub. Unmarried women dreamed. Matchmakers schemed.

All La Sembradora relished prospects of the upcoming event. Casinos clambered to hire the finest orchestras from Monterrey. Merchants dusted faded wares in anticipation. Restaurants printed special menus. The mayor issued orders to drench the village plaza in paper flowers.

Women fussed in frenzy about what to wear. For days, Eva and I poured through fashion magazines and every sewing pattern in Mamá's collection. One afternoon, just weeks before the bullfight, we sat on the floor in my room studying magazines we'd spread out around us.

"What do you think of this one?" I dangled a pattern for a purple gown inches from Eva's nose. She fanned her fingers in the air, scrunched her nose.

"It's hideous, Inma! We're not going to a masquerade ball." With that came the gentle toss of her head and spirited laughter that endeared her to everyone. She rolled her eyes and unfurled a teasing smile. "I found mine!" She waved a gossip magazine.

I snatched it from her, gawked at the images on the page and giggled. In one picture, Jorge Negrete, a popular singer and movie actor, in full mariachi attire, held up an arm to block an open-handed slap from an elegantly dressed temptress. I blinked at her outfit. She wore a tailored dress with a scooped neckline, outlined in folds of fabric swept aside and fastened at the collar with rhinestone buttons. The folds cascaded over the shoulder to mid-back, like a fabric waterfall. I nodded in approval and marveled at how much the form-fitted bodice and straight skirt would complement Eva's slender figure. A pert hat with a single plume, elbow-length gloves and a brocade evening bag completed "the look" Eva longed to duplicate. "Good choice, *prima*!" I said.

"Where can I get a hat like that?" she whined.

"I know! We'll pluck a feather from Mamá's rooster."

"*Ya,* Inma, you're not so funny."

"*Ay,* look at this one. It's me!" I spotted my choice in another magazine—a sweet, lace-trimmed, hip-snug chemise, its wide sash confettied with tiny fabric flowers, the skirt draped in tender pleats to just below the knee. "What do you think, *prima*?"

"Saucy!" Eva grinned.

"*Pero* very feminine…enchanting, really, don't you think?"

"It's a bit old-fashioned. A chemise, Inma? *Por favor.*"

"I think it's alluring."

"Maybe so, in a quaint sort of way," she said.

"Look at the accessories!" I sighed. The model peeked from under a wide-brimmed hat, its veil showered with fabric petals. Her hands, clad in short, pearl-clasped gloves, clutched an embroidered pouch to her lap. "They're perfect!" I said.

"*Ay, prima,* you are such an *inocente.*" Eva shook her head and smiled.

Later we joined Mamá in her bedroom to choose fabrics for our dresses. She always provided us with supplies from her dry goods collection. She smiled and pulled out bolt after bolt of exquisite satins, rayon crepes, silks and organzas from an armoire that guarded such treasures. Eva and I studied each roll, and contemplated transformations.

"I like that one!" Eva pointed at a mauve crepe.

"That's a good choice for the cut of your dress," Mamá said as she draped some of the fabric around my cousin.

"*¡Ay*, Tía, *mil gracias!*" Eva hugged her.

"Mamá, I want this one." I yanked at a roll of beige silk.

"*¡Inma, por favor!*" Eva's eyebrows arched. "You'll look like you're going to your First Holy Communion."

"It's not white!" I turned to study my mother's face.

"*Sí, hija*, you're right. *Pero* the style of your dress calls for more color."

"Like what?" I frowned.

"Maybe this coral silk. And I'll fashion some tiny flowers from this yellow organza to decorate it."

"I like my first choice better." I pouted.

Eva shook her head. "*Por Dios*. You'll get that white thing soiled before we get out the front door."

"It's not white! Tell her, Mamá," I pleaded.

Mamá held up her hand. "I'm afraid I have to agree with your *prima*. The coral is more practical. And more beautiful." She tilted her head aside. "Look in the mirror." She draped the coral fabric across my shoulders.

"*Ay*, Tía, I love it!" Eva said. "Inma, you've got to admit it's gorgeous. And the color is lovely on you."

I blinked at my reflection. "It *is* pretty."

"And the organza flowers will complement it perfectly. You'll see. I won't disappoint you." Mamá's eyes searched my face.

"Of course not. You're the best seamstress ever." I smiled.

"Wait, I almost forgot. I've got a surprise for you girls." Mamá set the fabric aside, pulled a cardboard box from the armoire and opened it.

"Stockings?" I said. "For us?"

Mamá nodded. She handed me the box marked, "Lé Mode, Real Silk Stockings", and smiled. "Go on! Each of you, take a pair."

"*¡Ay, muchas gracias, Tía!*" Eva said.

"I love you, Mamá! You're the best!" I bounced up and down. Eva joined in.

"Stop, girls! Enough! I must get back to work." She glanced toward the store and turned on her heel.

"When can you start the dresses?" I called after her.

She surrendered arms to the air and said, "I suppose I could tonight." She turned at the door and faced us. "You two see about getting some accessories. Don't worry about the dresses. No need to panic. At least, not yet." She grinned, shook her head and walked away.

Eva and I looked at each other askance.

"How are we ever going to afford new hats, gloves and evening bags?" I said.

"And shoes," Eva sighed.

"And shoes," I echoed.

A sly smile stole across Eva's face. "I know! We'll get Lola to lend us whatever we want. She has so many fancy things."

"You can't mean your sister Lola?"

"Who else? You've seen all the nice things she has."

"Of course. Everyone knows she's the best-dressed girl in town. She must spend her entire paycheck on clothes. *Pero*, Eva, you know how particular she is. She'll never let us borrow her things!"

"Don't worry, I'll make her. I've got enough on her to fill a closet."

"What do you mean?"

"Never mind, Inma. Just trust my word. She owes me."

"*Ay*, Eva, you know she'll throw a tantrum."

"Don't be such a fraidy cat! Think of all her nice things and how we can choose whatever we want."

I gazed in Eva's direction. I envisioned an open armoire, replete with Lola's treasures, flashing an invitation to a fashion El Dorado loaded with shimmer. Blinded by the prospects, I blurted, "Let's do it!"

"Of course we will. Now we just plan the ambush," Eva purred.

Chapter Three: Girls Just Want to Dress Up

The next afternoon, Eva and I sat in her bedroom and waited for Lola to leave for work.

"How long will she be gone?" I asked.

"Hours! Plenty of time for us to select things and try them on."

"Are you certain she's going to work?" I insisted.

"What do you mean? Of course she is. It's Tuesday!" Eva rolled her eyes.

"Isn't she free one afternoon a week?"

"*Ay, prima*, quit being such a worry wart," Eva said. She went to the door and peeked down the hallway.

"You're not certain what her schedule is, are you?" I stood up, hands on hips.

My cousin turned to look at me. "Would you quit worrying! I swear you are quite the naïve one." She patted me on the shoulder, cocked her head aside and shrugged like a comical marionette. She lifted and dropped her shoulders over and over, arms stiff.

I flopped onto the bed and giggled. "Enough, you clown. I'll lose my lunch!"

"Go ahead, see if I care. I'll just leap out of the way." Eva hopped around the room, bouncing and flinging her arms in the air.

I struggled to sit upright. "*Ay*, Eva, *por favor*. I'm serious. My stomach truly aches from laughing. Besides, we aren't listening. Lola may already have left."

"A lot you know. She always calls out to Mamá when she's leaving."

"Okay, smarty pants, *pero* I still don't see how you expect to get away with this. Lola will realize some things are missing the moment she returns." I raised my eyebrows at Eva.

"Ah, who knows? Lola's got so much, she may not."

"What about when she sees us at the *tardeada*?" I searched Eva for any sign of nervousness. "What will we do then?" I asked. She didn't blink.

"Who cares? Lola can't touch us, I tell you."

"What are you talking about? She'll make a scene. I'm sure of it. *Ay, prima*, can you imagine what an *escándalo*? She'll embarrass us in front of everyone."

"Inma, details, details! I can handle her. Don't you fret. She owes me."

"Then why not just tell Lola we need to borrow a few things?"

"What, and spoil all the fun?" Eva grinned.

"Just what have you got on her? It better be enough to keep her quiet. It's not about how she sneaks out of the house without your father's permission, is it? That won't do. He already knows!"

She shook her head. "Something much juicier." She extended an arm as if to receive a kiss on the wrist and tilted back her head in a haughty farce.

"Eva, I hope you know what you're doing. Remember, Lola's already out in society and you're not. You're only fourteen!"

"I'll never be presented if Papá discovers I lie for my sister and, uh, her friend."

"Ah, and who might that be?" I waited. Eva said nothing. "You must tell me if I'm to take part in this awful business," I insisted.

"*Ay*, you are so dramatic, Inma. You can simply say you know who he is, if you're confronted. You don't have to reveal a name."

"*Pero*, of course, you *do* know it. Tell me, *prima*, who is it?"

"Come now, Inma, surely you can guess for yourself who he is. Who's been at her side most often at the plaza on Sunday afternoons?"

"I don't know. Everyone walks in groups."

"That's true, but after all we little 'chaperones' wander off to the *nevería* for ice cream sundaes, those groups dissolve into couples. Anyway, Lola pairs off with Juan de Dios, if you must know."

"*¡Ave María!* You can't mean Juan de Dios Tragón, that *ranchero* who drinks too much?"

"The very one." She lifted her chin in mock defiance. "She may run off with him for all I know."

"*Por Dios*, Eva. She'll be disgraced!"

"My sister is the least of my concerns. She's always fended quite well for herself. She can just stay at that barren ranch with her drunkard if society rejects her, for all I care. My concern is for poor Papá. Can you imagine? He'll simply faint!" Eva fell ramrod onto the bed.

I shook my head. "It's just like you to poke fun at something even as grave as this. Why, your father could have a heart attack for all you know. Just think. The family name will be dishonored...his business, his standing in the community...it will all come tumbling down. He's worked so hard, Eva. And what about your mother? She won't be able to face her friends."

"Inma, *por favor*, don't exaggerate. Mamá and her snobby friends will survive. They are all in cahoots with each other about secret *aventuras* from back in their own day! Did you know Doña Perfecta, Miss High Society herself, had a shotgun wedding?"

40

"Who doesn't? Unbelievable, isn't it?" I said. "She puts on such airs. *Pero*, Eva, you're up to your old tricks. You're trying to change the subject."

"Am not. I'm just saying there's nothing to worry about. Besides, Lola changes boyfriends at least once a season. You watch. When the summer fiestas begin, she'll trade in Juan de Dios for someone who can stand long enough to dance with her. Papá will never find out about this...unless you say something."

"You know me better than that! *Ay*, Eva, the very thought of Juan de Dios stumbling around the casino with Lola frightens me."

"She's too smart for that. They sit when he's had too much." Eva smirked.

I frowned. "I can't understand what she sees in him. He's not even handsome."

Eva bounced up from the bed and sang, "Lola loves Juan de Dios, Lola loves Juan de Dios!" She giggled. "What do you say to that, *prima*?"

"Shh! I hear something!" I said. The sound of heels tapping down the corridor grew louder, then seemed to evaporate into the distance.

Eva scrambled to the door, peeked out and hissed, "She's leaving!"

"*Adiós*, Mamá," Lola called from the doorway.

"*Vaya con Dios, hija.*" My aunt sounded drowsy.

The door clicked shut. "Let's go!" Eva waved for me to follow.

I tiptoed after her. She looked over her shoulder and laughed. "I wish you could see how silly you look! Mamá's gone back to her siesta, I'm sure, and no one else is here! You're acting like a burglar."

"*Pues*, I feel like one." I squinted at Eva and stuck out my tongue. By the time we reached Lola's room, we were both giggling uncontrollably. We doubled over in our mirth and shoved at each other.

"Stop it," I pleaded. "Let's hurry."

Eva rolled her eyes and bowed. "Whatever you wish, Madame."

"Where's the key?" I asked.

"Right here!" She reached atop the armoire, moved her hand around and said, "That's odd."

"What is it? You can't find the key? I knew it!" I shook my head.

"Ah, what's this?" She smiled, opened her hand flat and held the key to my face.

"Eva, I swear, this is making me queasy. We must concentrate. Quit playing *la loca*!" I said.

"How *loca* is this?" She stared at me as she turned the key and opened the armoire. "Ta-dah!"

I blinked at the glare of Lola's evening collection and froze as Eva tossed things onto the bed and floor.

"Hurry! Help me carry these...we'll try them on in my room," she said.

"*Pero* you've taken everything but the dresses!"

"Of course. The more to choose from, the better. It'll be fun. Let's go." She piled three hats on her head and scooped an armload of shawls, evening bags and shoes off the floor. I spread wide my arms, hunched over the goodies on the bed and gathered them tight against my chest. I took a deep breath and hurried after her.

When we reached Eva's room, we gleefully dumped everything onto the bed and started yanking at things. We tried on hats, gloves and shoes then tossed them back to the bed or at each other. We took turns marveling at our reflections in the mirror, smiling at some, frowning at others. We wobbled around the room in Lola's high heels and pointed at each other.

"Ooh, la, la, prima!" I nodded approval when Eva donned a bright red shawl.

"Not that one!" She flicked a white hat from my head and laughed.

"Eva, this is such fun! I feel like we're shopping in Paris," I said.

"Nothing as exotic as all that, I assure you, my dear." Nose upturned, Eva waved an arm clad in a black satin glove.

I flipped off a pair of shiny heels, leaned on the bed and laughed.

Eva snapped her fingers in my face. "Stop, *prima*! What do you think? Do you love it?" She struck a dramatic pose in the red hat and satin heels.

"You look like a movie star!" I sighed.

Eva squinted and shook her head.

"*Ay*, Eva, don't you believe me? You know you're pretty!" I said.

"Hee-haw, hee-haw!" Eva scrunched her nose at me. "A pretty little piggy pouts...hee-haw, hee-haw."

"You mean, oink, oink," I said, then whinnied like a horse and pranced about the room after her. Eva jumped onto the bed and bounced. Hats, shoes, bags levitated, plummeted, up and down. She was still bouncing when the bedroom door swung open. I gulped for air at the sight of Eva's sister.

Lola screamed, "What the DEVIL are you doing?" She stomped into the room angrily and scowled at us. She gazed at all the hats, gloves and shoes strewn about the room. "Are these...*MY* things?" she asked, dumbfounded. "WHAT WERE YOU THINKING?" she demanded.

"*Ay*, calm down," Eva returned. "We need to borrow some of these to match our dresses for the big *tardeada*, that's all."

"Oh, I see! You *need*! And why in all creation would I let you even touch any of my things? You give me that hat right now before I knock it off!" Lola clawed at the air.

Eva hopped off the bed. "Come now, dear sister of mine, all we need are shoes and hats. Tía's making our dresses," she sniffed.

"Don't forget purses and gloves, Eva," I murmured.

Lola paced around the room, gathered hats, evening bags and gloves from the bed and off the floor. "NEVER!" she howled. "And I'm telling Mamá on you. I can't believe this! How dare you sneak into my room behind my back! You are in trouble, Eva. You too, Inma!" She glared at me as she plucked a hat from my head.

"Not as much as you'll be if you tell Mamá." Eva spun around the room sporting Lola's fancy shawl. I watched its silky fringe flutter about in a dizzying dance.

"Stop it! Stop it! Give me that!" Lola screamed. She charged at Eva. I slinked toward the door.

"Catch, Inma!" Eva laughed. She rolled up the shawl and threw it toward me. The frilly thing unfurled in mid-air and landed, full veil, on Lola's head. She thrashed about and jerked it off her face. Eva howled with laughter. I clasped my hands over my mouth and giggled.

Lola jumped up and down shrieking, "¡Mamá, Mamá!" I felt goose bumps sprout on the back of my neck.

"Quit yelling," Eva said. "Face it, Lola, I can get you in more trouble than you can me. Remember, I know about you and Juan de Dios, that *diablo* of a man you sneak around with."

Lola sucked in a huge gasp. "You wouldn't!" She blinked at Eva and me.

"*Ah, pero* certainly I would." Eva lifted her chin. "After all, I'm risking my hide to keep your little secret. Surely you can do something for me in return."

"How could you do this to me?" Lola sobbed.

"Just lend us a few of these fancy things, and I won't tell on you." Eva bared her teeth at Lola, then turned to me. "And neither will Inma. Right, *prima*?" I nodded and grinned sheepishly.

"You...you are pure evil," Lola hissed. "I work so hard to buy pretty things. You *huercas* will ruin everything."

"Lola...*po..por favor*...I...ah...I promise we'll take good care of them," I ventured with a shrug.

"*Ay*, of course, you would say that. *Pero* how could I ever wear my things after everyone's seen them on you two...*esquinclas*. You don't understand!" she said.

"Such drama! You flatter yourself. Nobody cares what you wear. Half the time you go off with Juan de Dios, anyway!" Eva taunted.

"I'll break it off with him. That's what I'll do. You'll see!" Lola said.

"Ah, so that's the extent of your true love, ¿*no*? Then you lied to him, too. I'll tell everyone on you. Even him! How you'd rather hug your clothes than your boyfriend. Is that what you want?" Eva waited.

"How mean and horrid! You should be ashamed of yourself!" Lola narrowed her eyes at her sister.

"*Ya, ya, ya,* stop your insults. Tell me, then, how do you want to do this?" Eva tapped her foot. "You share the goods or you get grounded. Sounds like an easy choice to me. Right, Inma?"

"I know! Why don't we let Lola choose what we can borrow?" I said.

"*Por Dios, prima.* We wear what we want or no deal. Understood, Lola?" Eva stared at her sister.

"You better watch out, Eva. This will come back to haunt you. God will punish you!" Lola's voice trembled.

"Don't bring God into this. He knows your sins. Ha!" Eva tossed back her head and chuckled.

Lola glowered at us. "First let me see what you want to borrow. Then I'll decide."

"*Ay, tú,* I don't know how you got through elementary school," Eva volleyed. She looked at me, "*Bueno*, Inma, what'll it be?"

I shrugged. "I don't know."

"We want to see everything," Eva declared. "You might as well take your siesta, Lola. And why aren't you at work, anyway?"

"It's my afternoon off, if you must know. And I'm not leaving!"

"Suit yourself. Come on, Inma, let's try things on and decide what we want."

Chapter Four: Bad Omen for the Big Day

"Shame on you! Wake up, Inma!...Inma!" I opened my eyes to see Eva floating around my room, opening each window. She sang, *"Buenos días"* to someone on the sidewalk who approached Mamá's store.

I tossed about and pulled the covers over my head.

"Don't pretend. I know you're awake! Come on, *prima*, get up," Eva wailed. I lay still. She plopped onto the bed and leaned toward me.

"Boo!" I said and bolted upright. "I know, I know. This is it. Today's the day. The big *tardeada* at last. *Pero* we've got all day to get dressed."

"No, we don't!" Eva shook her head. "We have to be ready for the bullfight by three o'clock."

"The bullfight?" I asked. "We don't have tickets..." I watched Eva bite back a grin. "Rico got us tickets, didn't he? Didn't he?" I exclaimed. "But how? I thought they were sold out."

"Shh." Eva smiled wide. "Who knows? Of course he got us tickets. What else? I knew he would."

"Did you ask him to?"

"Inma! You know me better than that. Rico always spoils us."

"Only because he's in love with you." I looked at my beautiful cousin and shook my head.

"*Ay, niña,* such a child. You've got so much to learn. Don't you see? For men like Rico it's all about appearances…you know, high society and all that. It wasn't enough to take us to the *tardeada*," Eva said.

"I'm just glad he takes us everywhere."

"Come now, Inma, get dressed. We'll be late to La Cleopatra's."

I moaned, "I only wish we could afford La Cleopatra. Go sit at the vanity and we can pretend she's doing our hair."

"No, Inma! We've got appointments! Can you believe it? Rico!"

"No! And you accepted?" I hesitated. "Does Mamá know? I mean, tickets to a bullfight is one thing, *pero*…going to an expensive beauty salon is quite another matter."

"We won't mention it then." Eva smiled.

"How are we going to explain fancy hairdos?" I waved my hands about my head.

"Inma, Inma, what would you do without me? Just tell her we're going to el Salón Baratón. Tell her we saved up."

"Eva, Eva, you're not so smart. She'll know we're lying because we can do a better job than that awful place."

"*Ay*, we're wasting time. Tell her whatever you wish, *pero,* let's go. Now!"

After I dressed, Eva traipsed behind me to the store. Mamá handed a customer change, then turned to us. "So the big day is here, girls…what is it, Inma?"

"Nothing, Mamá. It's just that Eva and I have to hurry. We have an appointment at, uh, el Salón Baratón."

"*Pero* you girls do such a fine job on each other's hair. Why not play beauty salon here?" Mamá stared at me, then at Eva. "Inma! Where are you really going? You can't fool me, *hija*. Did Rico arrange something for you girls?"

I gasped. "Mamá! How did you know?"

"I always know when you're up to something." Mamá frowned, then sighed and shook her head. "And I know Rico. This is a big occasion for him."

"Please don't be angry," I said. "We have appointments with La Cleopatra, *pero* we won't go if you don't want us to." I hung my head.

"Inma!" Eva whimpered.

"Go on, both of you. This is a very special day." Mamá sounded distant.

"*Ay, gracias*," I said.

"*Pero* there's no need to lie, Inma, ever," my mother continued. "Always remember that. It may be difficult for you to realize that I was once a young girl myself." She smiled. "*Bueno, muchachas*, lunch is at noon. See that you're back in time. You'll stay for lunch, Eva?"

54

"*Sí*, Tía, *gracias*." Eva blushed. "You're the best. We're going to La Cleopatra's! Can you believe it?" She smiled at my mother.

"*Ah, qué Rico*. I'm not surprised. Have fun, girls." Mamá turned to greet her next customer.

Our neighbor, Doña Inez, shuffled into the store. Her eyebrows rounded almost to her scalp. "Are you two young ladies going to the big *tardeada* this evening?" she asked.

Eva and I nodded. The gnarled old woman focused on Eva. "I'm sure you'll be the most beautiful girl there." She nodded and turned to look at me. She flashed a toothless smile and warned, "Enjoy your youth, girls. *Pues*, before you know it, your bloom wilts on the vine and..."

"What can I get you?" Mamá interrupted.

Doña Inez's gaze remained on Eva and me. "I need an egg and a cup of sugar. The fortune teller is coming to heal me for a bad case of nerves. She says I have the fright, a bad case of *susto*. Yesterday she read my cards. They foretold something evil will happen today. I got so frightened that now she has to do a treatment."

"*Ay*, Doña, I wish you wouldn't believe everything that woman tells you," Mamá said. She glanced at us. "The girls were just leaving."

The old woman nodded. "Have fun, *muchachas*."

"*Sí, este, gracias*. Come on, Eva. We'll be back for lunch, Mamá," I said over my shoulder as we headed out the door.

"*Vayan con Dios*," Mamá sighed her blessing.

"That woman scares me," I said to my cousin as soon as we left the house.

"She's harmless enough, I think," Eva said.

"*Pero*, what the devil do you think will happen today?"

"Nothing, of course. The fortune teller just wants more money. I swear, Inma...you are such an *inocente*," Eva chided.

"*Ay tú*, Señorita Perfecta. Never mind that old woman. Let's go get glamorous!" I said.

Chapter Five: Glamour is as Glamour Does

When we walked into La Cleopatra's salon, everyone looked up. Busy chatter stopped. Clicking scissors froze mid-air. A nail file clinked onto the marble floor. A young girl hurried toward us.

"What is it?" she asked in a hushed voice while she looked us up and down.

"We have appointments," I said. "She's Eva and I'm Inmaculada."

The girl rolled her eyes. "Wait here." Instead of consulting the leather notebook on the front desk, she hurried off. Everyone watched as she disappeared behind a red velvet curtain, only to hurry out and slink back toward us. Activity resumed in frenzy, and gossip grew hushed as she approached us.

"*Ay,* forgive me, it's just that you are so...*pues,* so young! La Cleopatra awaits." She motioned toward the back of the salon. "She'll do your hair," she said to Eva, "while I do your nails." She pointed at me. "Then you'll switch places." She managed a broad smile and injected a weak lilt into an otherwise dull voice. "I forgot. *Bienvenidas a* La Cleopatra's. I am here to...uh, to serve you." She winced. "My name is Elegancia."

57

"*Mucho gusto.*" Eva giggled, stared her up and down. I nudged Eva to stop.

"Follow me, *por favor.*" Elegancia turned and fixed her gaze on the floor as she led us away.

"*Sí, vamos,* we need to hurry or we'll be late to the bullfight," I announced as we walked through the salon, then whispered to my cousin, "Eva, can you believe this? We're at La Cleopatra's!"

"Ah, and we've only begun to bloom!" Eva beamed as we paraded after Elegancia. As we parted, Eva whispered to me, "*Oye,* make friends with La Elegante. Maybe she makes house calls." I chuckled and nodded.

"Have a seat." Elegancia pointed to a burgundy armchair. I balked for a moment then complied when she took her place on a small black bench. She reached behind a satin curtain, rolled out a manicure table and positioned it between us. I marveled at the vast nail polish collection before me—mauve, pink, coral, cherry-red and *nacarado*, a rich tan, my favorite.

I watched Elegancia squint as she worked. "You're doing a really nice job," I offered. No response. I plowed ahead. "Did you do your own nails? They look pretty."

"*Ay, gracias.* You know the secret to a good manicure is that you have to file across the nail in only one direction. Like this." As she filed, she told me she'd worked at La Cleopatra's salon for five years. "She looks down her nose at everyone. *Pero* I have to help my mother," Elegancia continued. "My father's a good-for-nothing. Before I got this job, my mother didn't even have money to buy *frijoles* sometimes."

"My father died," I murmured, but Elegancia continued as if she hadn't heard me.

"I quit school because my mother embarrassed me in front of the other students," she said. "One day, my boyfriend José walked me home from school. Suddenly, we saw my mother coming toward us. She did not approve of José. I could tell right off she was angry. She'd been to the market and was carrying a bag full of vegetables. She screamed at José and me, reached into her shopping bag and threw tomatoes and *calabazas* at us. In front of everyone! When José got hit in the face with a tomato he ran away. The kids howled with laughter. I was so humiliated. You can imagine my shame. *¡Que vergüenza!*"

Elegancia slumped her head aside and stared at me. Her bottom lip quivered. Her eyelids fluttered. "You understand, don't you?"

I nodded and covered my mouth with one hand. I camouflaged a giggle with an onslaught of pretend cough noises that led to a series of true attempts to clear my throat. "Uh-hum, so what did your mother do then?"

"*Pues*, she scooped up what was left of the vegetables and tossed them into her shopping bag while she called me bad names. I wanted to die right there! All the kids saw everything. I know they did! I could hear them laughing all the way home. Anyway, I never went back to school."

"*Ay, pues*, Elegancia, some kids make fun of me for selling candy at school..."

"I knew you'd understand." She sighed, "I could never live down something like that. To this day, I can't tolerate criticism against anyone. I just can't. *Pero* here at La Cleopatra's, I'm forced to listen and smile as customers gossip and criticize everyone in town. What else can I do? I need the money. I'm saving for..."

My mind wandered as she droned on. I glanced around the shop at hairdressers fussing over their customers. Thick clouds of hair spray spurted here and there over the chattering women. The smell of permanent-wave lotion hung heavy in the air.

"Did you hear me?" Elegancia demanded. I turned to face her frown.

"Of course!" I nodded and grinned.

Elegancia pouted. "A friend of mine came by this morning and gave me news of my mother. It seems a fortune teller warned her something evil will happen today. She's beside herself with fright. I can't believe she gives her money to that witch! Her money, ha! That's money I send her. And she wastes it on such witchcraft, such *brujerías*...what is it?" Elegancia looked at me. "You look surprised."

"Nothing, really," I answered. "It's just that you're the second person who's told me that something terrible will happen today."

"Who else told you? Who?"

"*Pues*, it was my neighbor, Doña Inez."

"That's my mother! You see how she is! She's telling everyone in town. She never shuts up and it's always bad news. That's why I had to move out. What with her complaining and my *borracho* father stumbling down sidewalks. I couldn't stay there. I'd rather live in the tiny room where La Cleopatra hides me while she entertains her gentlemen callers, if you know what I mean. I have to clean that whole *mansión* of hers. Ha, you should see the place. Just a stupid little house, only she decorates it all gaudy and everything, just like this place." She waved at the faux zebra-skin rug on the wall and the plastic chandelier overhead. "So you're my mother's neighbor," Elegancia said.

"Huh?" I was surprised she'd stopped talking.

"How small the world is. That's what I always say. I want to move to Villa Buena Aventura someday. I'm saving my money. Whatever I can from what La Cleopatra gives me. She says I should be happy because she feeds me. Ha! Most days it's just *frijoles* and *tortillas*. I can't wait to get away. *Oye*, do me a favor and don't tell my mother you met me. Anyway, you're done. Just in time, too. Here comes your friend. Is she as stuck up as she acts?" Elegancia raised her chin in Eva's direction.

"No, no, she just likes to have fun with everyone. You know, *muy chistosa*. She doesn't mean any harm. Just teases. She's my cousin, a *prima hermana*."

"What are you saying about me?" Eva sang as she strolled up.

"Guess what, Eva. Elegancia is Doña Inez's daughter," I said as I fanned my freshly polished fingernails in Eva's direction.

"*Por favor*, don't tell anyone else!" the manicurist pleaded.

"*Ay*, forgive me," I said. "It's just that I tell Eva everything."

My cousin rolled her eyes. "We won't tell anyone your secret," she said to Elegancia. She looked at me, puzzled, and said, "My, how small the world is...*ay, pero,* Inma, what about my hair! Do you love it?"

I looked up. "Wow! Eva, it's stunning! Turn around. Let me see the back. *Ay, qué hermoso.*" Eva's hair was swept into a French twist that started from the nape of her neck like the tip of a tornado and spun wider as it followed the contour of her head to a bed of curls on top. Tiny ringlets framed her face. Rhinestone butterflies hovered like magic all over her hair. Her face glowed in shades of pink and purple. "Eva, you look like a movie star, like Dolores del Río!" I beamed.

"*Ay,* stop it! Don't make fun of me, *prima.*" She laughed.

"*Sí,* like Dolores del Río," Elegancia insisted. "You look just like her. She is so beautiful. I mean, even though she's more fair-skinned, you are still prettier, I think. "

Eva shrugged. "*Ay, gracias a Dios,* I guess. *Pero, chica,* do me a favor, let's hurry. Let me see, I want lavender nails. Do you have that color?" she said.

"*¿Cómo?* " Elegancia asked.

"Lavender, you know—violet, light purple."

"*Sí,* of course I have lavender." She looked around. "It's not here. I bet the other manicurist has it. Excuse me. I'll be back as soon as I can. I won't be long. She's always taking my things. She's such a thief. I know…" Elegancia's voice faded as she shuffled away.

Eva rolled her eyes. "She's just like her mother with all the gossip. I'll have to stare at a magazine while she does my nails. I hope she won't talk the entire time."

"You know she will," I replied. Eva and I were still laughing when Elegancia returned.

"I found one. Look how pretty," she said, holding up a bottle of nail polish. "*Oye,* Inmaculada," she said to me, "La Cleopatra asked for you. Don't keep her waiting or she'll make you ugly." Elegancia giggled, then pointed. "She's behind that thick red curtain."

Elegancia turned to Eva and signaled for her to be seated. "Lavender is a good choice for you," she said. "*Bueno,* any of them would be great on you. *Pero* it's the manicure that counts. You have to file the nail in one direction like this. That's the key to a good manicure. That, and how you push back the cuticles. I can always tell…"

I bared my teeth in a mock grin at my cousin.

"Get me a magazine before you go, Inma!" Eva's eyebrows shot up.

"No time." I flapped both hands in her face. "Look, I chose *nacarado*."

Elegancia did not pause for breath. I heard her say something about her mother again as I walked away.

*   *   *

"So you're Inmaculada," La Cleopatra purred. "*Bienvenida*." She motioned for me to take a seat in front of a huge gilded mirror.

"*Gracias*, Doña Cleopatra." I grinned and eased into a fancy upholstered chair.

"*Ay, por favor*, call me Pati," she said. But she looked pure Cleopatra. Her smile unveiled gold frames around stark white teeth. Her hair was dyed blue-black and hung straight to the shoulders. Severe bangs lay like curtains to just above her eyebrows, which penciled black pyramids. Her eyelids were powdered cobalt blue and lined in thick black slants a full inch beyond the corner of her eyes. She wore a white satin gown. Gold viper bracelets wrapped around both her upper arms. Her lipstick shone purple. Her spider-like eyelashes fluttered as she gazed at my reflection in the mirror.

I gawked. She placed a satin wrap around me and patted my shoulder. I froze when she lifted my chin with her forefinger.

"Let's see." She leaned her head aside and narrowed her eyes. "You know, I think you'll look magnificent in an updo, and to add a glamorous touch, I'll pin all your hair to one side and fashion some curls from top to bottom. What do you think? You like the idea?"

I nodded so hard my chin hit my neck. "Sounds exotic."

"You'll look very special," she said. "We'll also do your makeup. Did you like your *prima's* look?"

I nodded. "Eva's beautiful."

"You are just as beautiful, *mija*. There are many kinds of beauty, believe me."

I grinned. "*Pero* Eva's the one all the boys seem to like."

"*All* the boys? Come now, I'm sure you have many admirers as well."

"Some, perhaps, *pero* not as many as Eva."

"Do you resent your *prima* for that?"

"*Ay, no.* I love her all the more. She doesn't take on airs about her beauty. She's so much fun to be with. The way I look at it, I meet more boys than I would without her."

"You are wise to understand that. *Pero* don't underestimate the power of your own charm. Beauty is not just hair and nails, although it certainly helps." La Cleopatra smiled as she brushed my hair. "You'll find that you get what you expect when it comes to men's reactions. Women who think they're beautiful get treated as if they truly are."

I nodded and squirmed a bit in my chair.

"I like to startle men with my image," she continued. "I expect to awe them, and I nearly always do. It keeps most of them at bay. That way, I only 'reel in' those I choose."

"How, uh…" I peered into her heavily lined eyes. "How do you do that?"

La Cleopatra chuckled deep in her throat. Her eyes twinkled as she methodically teased my hair. "*Pues*, I just give them a look that says, 'go away, closer.' If they respond appropriately, I know they're brave enough, and perhaps interested enough, to treat me with the respect I want from a man. You should try it sometime." She smoothed and pinned my hair deftly as she spoke.

"I, uh, sure...*pero*, how can I tell them to go away and come closer?" I said.

"It's quite simple. Just pierce their eyes with yours while you think, 'I wish you'd go away because I find you irresistible...danger ahead.' Watch...like this." She peered at herself in the mirror, narrowed her eyes and rolled a shoulder. "That's how I do it."

"Ah, I see." I nodded. "I'll have to practice that."

La Cleopatra tossed back her head and guffawed.

*   *   *

"Too much makeup! And those hairstyles! Too *exagerados*. Outlandish!" Mamá waved her arms.

"*Pero*, Tía, just think. La Cleopatra herself did our hair and makeup! Right, Inma?" Eva's eyes pleaded.

"That's right, Mamá. These are Paris styles."

"And that's where they belong! This is a small town. What will people say?"

"Only that they love the dresses you made us!" I sashayed over, hugged my mother tight and kissed her on the cheek. I looked at Eva and winked.

"Tía, all the women who were at La Cleopatra's today will be at the *tardeada*. We'll fit right in," Eva exclaimed.

"That's what I'm afraid of." Mamá sighed then turned away. "*Bueno, pues*, at least rub off some of that paint! *Por Dios*, you are young girls!"

As my mother walked out of the room, I shot a gleeful we-got-away-with-it look at Eva. She smiled, nodded and shuffled over to me. We held hands and spun around the room, two giddy children. Then we doubled over in giggles.

"Stop it, stop it, *prima*," I said. "Our hairdos! Quit making me laugh!"

"How, like this? Or this?" She poked at me.

"Eva, I'll ruin my makeup! *Basta ya*, I mean it."
I tried to sound serious, but whooshed out a loud, "Pfft!"
and roared with laughter when Eva charged at me. She
held two fingers, pretend bull's horns, over her head.

"Look out, look out! Here comes *el toro*," she
yelled. I moved aside and shoved her as she ran by. Her
eyes grew wide as she fell to the floor. I held my breath
until she rolled about chuckling.

"Eva, don't be such a clown," I pleaded

"I'm not a clown, Inma. I'm a *toro*." She smiled.

"Well, we're not going to see a real *toro* if we
don't hurry," I insisted.

"All right, spoilsport. *Pero* we're already
beautiful. All we have to do is slip into our dresses."

"Don't forget hats, gloves and shoes."

"I'm not wearing a hat," Eva said.

"You're not?"

70

"Come on now, I'm not about to cover La Cleopatra's artwork." Eva pointed at her head.

"I suppose you're right. We shouldn't hide our glamorous hairdos. *Pero* the hats we chose are so beautiful," I whined.

"*Ay Dios*, Inma. Don't be such a baby. We'll wear them some other time."

"We won't look complete without hats, Eva."

"So we'll wear flowers instead."

"Flowers?" I shook my head.

"What could be more perfect? Flowers in our hair for the bullfight and the *tardeada*. We'll look like beautiful women from Spain, *españolas*!"

"You mean we'll look like flamenco dancers," I said.

Eva shrugged. "Okay, we'll look like flamenco dancers. Exquisite ones!"

"Okay, and where do we get flowers?"

"How about the plaza? We'll cut some hibiscus."
Eva smiled.

"*Ay, sí*, and they'll wilt before we get to the bullring, you silly," I said.

Eva heaved a deep sigh. "*Bueno*, what about the ones in your parlor?"

"You mean Mamá's silk flowers? Eva!"

"*Ay, Dios*. We'll put them back." She shrugged.

"You certainly complicate my life, *prima*."

"*Ah, pero* it's so much fun." Eva flashed a toothy smile.

Chapter Six: Off to the Bullfights

"You're both lovely." Rico hummed his approval as we gingerly climbed into the back seat of his stunning 1936 Ford coupe. I stared at the bright *sarape* draped behind us and elbowed Eva. She crossed her eyes at me.

The driver shut the door and climbed into the car. "Wait until El Victor, the most famous matador in the entire world, lays eyes on the likes of you two!" Rico exclaimed.

Eva squeezed my knee and crossed her eyes again. I shook my head and covered my mouth to stifle a snicker. She giggled. "*Pues gracias*, Rico. If we get any compliments today it's because of La Cleopatra's talents. That was very kind of you."

"*Sí, gracias*, Rico," I piped in.

"The pleasure is all mine, *muchachas*." He chuckled. "Besides, I must confess I have very selfish motives." The driver coughed. Rico stared into the distance. "Perfect weather for an afternoon outdoors. I reserved box seats on the shaded side of the arena."

We arrived in style. Rico stepped out one side of the car and extended his arm to Eva. The driver opened the other door and offered me a hand. I wobbled in Lola's high heels but managed to steady myself. Rico crooked both elbows, a cue for us girls to take our places on either side of him and proceed.

"Eva, Eva, everyone's staring at us!" I hissed as we approached the bullring. "I'm afraid we overdid this flamenco notion of yours." I tugged at the sticky flower in my hair.

No reply from Eva other than a wide smile and nod. She tipped her head at one of the bullfighters, who stopped in his tracks as we neared the entrance.

"*Buenas tardes.*" He removed his cap and bowed.

"*Buenas tardes.*" A gruff retort from Rico seemed to startle the young man.

I grinned and shrugged my free shoulder at the bullfighter. He in turn swept aside and extended an arm in a dramatic gesture as if faced with some majestic bull. His stare never swayed from Eva. I sighed, pawed at the drawstring of my evening bag and fumbled about for my silk fan. Eva ignored the drooped *macho* and tilted her head so high I could see her nose hairs.

As we walked away, I studied the young matador. Finally, either the psychic energy of my stare or the sight of Eva's upturned nose drew his attention to me. His shriveled brows burrowed to a point at the bridge of his nose. His eyes pleaded. His jacket looked worn. A dark mole dangled at the tip of his impish nose. My playful lust cooled to mischievous pity. I lifted my fan in time to conceal a giggle. Rico tightened his grip on us as we strode ahead through the mob toward the stands. I glanced over my shoulder for one last look at the humbled *torero*. He stood in the same spot. His eyes grew wide at me while he dusted his suit. I shook my head.

We nudged our way toward the bullring through the raucous crowd. Most people walked in small clusters, peculiar bouquets of smell, color and sound—the full array of bullfight aficionados for miles around. The stench of sweat danced alongside the scent of exotic perfumes. Satin skirts swished, rustled, swung wide and, like so many brilliant bells, seemed to clang against the linen-clad legs of hacienda laborers who'd been granted the afternoon off by their *patrones*. Boisterous chatter, taunting catcalls, shrill whistles and booming laughter resounded near and far, a cacophony of hopeful expectations. Vendors hawked souvenir key chains and mementos, yelling loudly over the din.

Wide-brimmed sombreros alongside ladies' feathered hats bobbed and tossed about, a calliope of crests in the tides of excitement. The throng streamed toward a clogged entrance, then drained into human tributaries that divided the masses into their respective places in the scheme of things.

Mustachioed Emiliano Zapata look-alikes held tight their hats with calloused fingers as they hopped up the rickety, sun-bleached stairs to the loftiest splintered bleachers. *Rancheros* huddled together on the deck, puffed cigars and slapped each other on the back in hearty displays of manly *abrazos* and greetings of "*Hola, compadre.*"

The licorice stink of cigar smoke meshed in the air with that of stale cigarettes and assaulted my helpless nostrils. I fanned the stench away from my face.

Caballeros, gloved hands extended, escorted wives or lovers, who gripped their skirts as they teetered toward box seats. Bursts of laughter came from *ranchero* huddles whenever a skirt rose high enough to reveal more than the usual feminine charm.

Rico strutted tall, Eva and I on each elbow, like clinging porcelain teacups. He pointed to our ringside box. I gazed at the giant purple and green *sarapes* that draped the rail before our seats. Rico guided Eva and me to our cushioned positions on either side of him. Then he settled his ample posterior into the seat between us.

"Happy, *muchachas*?" He smiled.

"*Ay, sí, gracias,* Rico. This is *sooo* perfect," Eva chirped.

"*Sí,* this is *sooo* perfectly perfect." I echoed the sentiment and mimicked Eva.

"Only the best for you beautiful *señoritas.* After all, this is a grand occasion. El Victor himself will be right here today." He pointed to the orange sand directly below us.

I leaned back and tapped Eva's shoulder with my fan. "Within spitting distance," I whispered. "Close enough to see all the matadors eye-to-eye." Eva grinned, shook her head and held a finger to her lips, eyes riveted on Rico's back.

"Your beauty will inspire them." Rico drew a long sigh. He nodded toward Eva, then turned to me. "I expect you to behave like ladies today. You mustn't make your clown faces at the matadors, Inma. Promise?"

My eyes shot skyward. "Uh, what about at the bulls?"

Rico's laughter—a fit of clucks, hiccups and saliva spewed into the air. He clutched at his belly and shook his head.

Eva joined the pandemonium. She tossed back her head and howled. Rico stiffened. "*Muchachas*...let's behave...come now. What will people think?" He looked around. Some of the *rancheros* stared in our direction.

Suddenly a barrage of "tah-tah-tah-dah" trumpet blasts ripped through the air. Every eye in the stands riveted to the arena entrance. The band squawked out a march, while a parade of *banderilleros*, in bright costumes hugged firm against their svelte torsos, streamed, single file, into the bullring. They carried *banderillas*, brightly decorated wooden spears. Next came the *picadores* on horseback, proudly yielding lances at their sides. Each of the horses was shielded by a quilted wrap around the lower part of its body to protect it from bulls' horns.

The *banderilleros* strutted, straight-legged, pointed-toes forward, around the perimeter of the arena. Puffs of dust rose with every step the men took. Each of them saluted onlookers with one hand and twirled a *banderilla* with the other. The brightly decorated spears spun like brilliant butterflies in flight. The *picadores* bounced along next to the *banderilleros* and circled the arena. The afternoon's entertainment had begun!

The crowd roared. Many shot to their feet, waved arms overhead and raised a thunderous clamor. Riotous cheers, piercing whistles, and deafening *"¡Ajúa!"* *gritos* flooded the air. One wretched drunk tumbled down several rickety stairs and landed in the aisle next to me, where he tossed about in pain. He grunted, *"Ay...ay...ay."*

A couple of his cohorts jumped to his rescue, only to be cursed by the drunk when they tried to hoist him away. *"Orale,* what the devil? I came here to watch a bullfight, and I'm going to watch the darned bullfight. Can't you see I'm in pain? Leave me alone!"

Rico slapped his hands to his knees and snarled something incoherent. He pushed himself up, squared his shoulders and yanked at his tailored jacket. I stared as he squeezed past me to the aisle, where he towered over the sprawled man. Rico's formidable figure rendered a canopy that shaded the hapless drunk, whose mouth oozed saliva. The injured drunkard trembled. He looked around for his *compadres* as they backed away.

Rico glared at him. "Listen, you! I don't care if you're drawing your last breath. You will not watch the bullfight here. You'd better let your *amigos* cart you away before I kick your...let's see...where does it hurt most? Tell me!"

The old man cringed. His friends moved back another step, eyes wide.

I rubbed my hands together. "This is going to be good," I whispered to Eva. "Rico's imitation of a *macho*?" I said and smiled at my cousin. She grinned and turned back to the arena. I shrugged and stared at the showdown beside me.

One of the men came forward. "We'll take him...*por favor*...we want no problems." He gawked at Rico and hesitated.

"*Pues*, do it quickly. What are you waiting for, *hombre*?"

"*Vámonos*, Don Ebrio." The man's rescuers yanked him up by the armpits. He let out a loud belch as they lugged him away. Rico stamped his foot before he spun around and returned to his seat. I struggled to decipher his mumbled condemnations as he brushed past me and took his place. I turned to watch the men deposit Don Ebrio, kerplunk, on the walkway above us and scurry off, crouched low, to their seats.

"What an unfortunate slob!" I said and stared at Rico's somber profile. No response.

"Rico, look! That *banderillero* has turned into a statue." Eva pointed. "Over there, Inma."

Rico chuckled. "The poor imbecile appears to have fallen under your spell, Eva. What do you think? Let's dub him El Maniquí. He's become a mannequin!"

"*Ay*, Rico, you exaggerate," Eva cooed. She blinked and smiled at El Maniquí, who had stepped away from the compelling rotation of prancers to stand, soldier-straight, rooted before us, eyes fixed on my cousin.

As the *banderilleros* approached the transfixed dolt, their eyes followed his to Eva. They stepped around him in varying degrees of artful grace. Several glossy butterfly wings swooned during the eyes-right glances then recovered in altered courses—now fractured, perpendicular flaps rather than horizontal twirls. Yet, the other *banderilleros* managed to dart past the object of El Maniquí's attention.

I sucked in a deep breath, coughed and nudged Rico. "Can you believe this? Everyone's staring at us."

"Let them look…this is fun," he replied.

I looked down and bared my best scowl at El Maniquí. He didn't flinch. I gaped as the *banderilleros* continued to traipse, puppetlike, around the lovelorn fool.

"*Pero*, Rico, Eva will surely get the evil eye…we'll all get it!" I insisted.

"Nonsense. Don't be ridiculous. There's no such thing," he said.

"Ah, *pero* there certainly is! Happens to me all the time." I sniffed. No reply. I gawked at Eva's reaction to such a scandalous display. My blood rushed warm as I watched her nod, grin and wave at each of her admirers.

"Really, Eva. You're making a scene," I hissed.

Rico tapped me on the shoulder and motioned toward the arena. One of the men stood square behind El Maniquí, with the sharp end of a red *banderilla* poised mid-air, parallel to the hapless lover's posterior. Cries of encouragement tangled with jeers from the bleachers. I smiled wide.

With a jab, the weapon found its mark and ripped through El Maniquí's pants. The flesh and bone statue jumped, rubbed his rear end then heaved a parting sigh at Eva. He shuffled through the sand as he trudged behind his attacker, who hurled a hearty wave to onlookers. The crowd rumbled with laughter and derision.

"How embarrassing! I wouldn't find it flattering to entrance such a nitwit!" I said.

Eva turned in my direction. "I felt sorry for him, that's all," she said.

Rico interjected, "Girls, we are here to have a good time. Please try to get along. Inma, you mustn't be envious of Eva. No need for *envidias*."

"No sermon necessary, Rico," Eva said. "Inma and I tease each other all the time. Don't we, *prima*?" She leaned her head aside and crossed her eyes at me. I laughed. She beamed.

Chapter Seven: El Chico and a Scrawny Bull

An ear-splitting screech and a sharp "tap-tap" of the microphone brought our little drama to a halt. A deep voice reverberated in a series of explosive booms, crackles and echoes, *"Muy buenas...*(pshht) *tardes! Bienvenidos* ladies and (squawwk) gentle...men...I proudly (screeech) present...this afternoon's matadors!" Suddenly, the microphone went dead, but the announcer proceeded. He yelled loudly, "From Monterrey, Nuevo León, El Chico!"

A skinny young man strutted to the middle of the arena and raised his cap to the audience. He was greeted with cheers and whistles.

"From Mexico City," the announcer continued, "El Angel de la Muerte." A well-known figure throughout Mexico, this bullfighter, better known as La Muerte, received a warmer, louder welcome from the crowd. But when El Victor was introduced next, everyone in the stands rose to their feet, stomped, whistled and cheered so that the stands shook.

Eva and I craned our necks for a better view. "He's so handsome," I said. "I wonder what color his eyes are?"

"I can't tell. Maybe we'll get a better look later so you can find out!" Eva giggled.

Each of the matadors wore a brilliant "suit of lights" with elaborate embroidery designs and sequins on satin. None was as elegant as that of El Victor, which was made of white satin and gold trim.

Other *toreros*, the bullfighters' helpers, joined the three matadors and together the men marched across the bullring to the officials' box, where they formally greeted the president of the bullfight then proceeded around the perimeter of the arena, smiling and waving at spectators. The crowd went wild when El Victor and La Muerte exited the arena through the same gate they had entered. El Chico took his place behind the protective wood *barrera* to one side of the arena and waited for the first bullfight to be announced.

When his name was called, the scrawny matador leapt to the center of the arena in arrow-straight kicks, his cape flapping behind him. Some fans rallied to their feet. Others blinked momentarily at the knock-kneed young man and resumed their boisterous chatter. Trumpets sounded with each bounce El Chico took. He raised his cap, executed a dramatic pirouette and swan-dived from the waist down, one arm outstretched.

"I've never heard of this kid," Rico mumbled.

El Chico continued his ballet in a series of prances and pirouettes around the entire bullring.

"What a showboat!" Rico said. "Who does this clown think he is? Why, he's an unknown."

"Perhaps he'll dance his way around the bull." I giggled. Rico smiled.

People in the stands bellowed curses between cupped hands. A huge wave of groans lapped around the arena and grew louder with every leap the matador took. He finally turned his attention away from the air above his nose and peered at the restless spectators. Some held their noses and flapped their arms at him. Others tossed beer bottles, peanuts and candy wrappers into the arena.

El Chico stopped short and in solemn, stiff gait, head held high, marched toward the *barrera* that would shield him from the bull and, at least momentarily, from raucous onlookers. The band heaved a shaky beat, followed by a hectic drum roll. The noise in the stands subsided. Quickly, the announcer's voice telegraphed the name of the bull through the microphone squeaks and static.

"Never heard of the bull either," Rico scoffed. "El Flaco Feroz. Skinny and fierce? What a joke of a name!"

The gates flew open and the lean bull scrambled out. Everyone cheered. The bull dashed in jolts about the arena, jerked its horns from side to side then stopped on the shaded side of the arena. El Chico stepped out from behind the *barrera*, huge bright cape held high before him, and approached the bull in measured steps.

The matador stopped several yards from the beast, which stared blankly at the cape and wagged its head. El Chico shook the cape and grunted, "*Aja, toro. ¡To...ro!*" The bull turned and walked away from the matador's satin taunt. Loud laughter and catcalls rained from the stands. The lanky matador scurried after the bull.

This time he stood closer and brushed the cape against the bull's nose. "*Aja, to...ro.*" The bull nudged its horns into the cape, lifting the satin into the air. The bull ambled under it. Massive disgust thundered from the bleachers.

"What a useless bull they gave the poor fellow!" Rico said. "*Pero* a matador worth his weight can make even a lazy bull charge."

"I don't think he has enough weight," I sighed. Rico snickered. I smiled and nodded at Eva.

She sneered, "Maybe he'll surprise you…Look! You see."

El Chico and El Flaco Feroz now spun, one on either side of the cape like a colorful top in the sand. Murmured *"olés"* swept round, like a gentle breeze, then a brisk wind that encircled man and beast in a faster dance. Weave, *"¡olé!"*, twist, *"¡olé!"*, swirl, *"¡OLÉ!"*, spin, *"¡OLÉ!"*

Suddenly, the bull stopped and bumped its partner aside. El Chico stumbled. He teetered on one foot, then hopped and planted down the other in a sort of jig. He gawked at the bull, which blinked, motionless. The matador strutted away and saluted onlookers. A smattering of applause trickled from the audience. Some people waved back. Most resumed their conversations or called out to vendors for more food and drink.

El Chico twirled his cape about in a dramatic show for spectators. Meanwhile, El Flaco Feroz raised his head, pawed at the ground then charged toward the commotion. The flamboyant matador's eyes whipped over his shoulder as he swished the cape away from his body. As El Chico reeled about, the bull's left horn ripped through his pants. A thin line of blood zigzagged across the matador's thigh. He folded into the dust and rolled away from the bull.

Screams electrified the arena. Several *toreros* rushed, capes forward, to distract the bull from the writhing man. The band squawked to life. El Chico struggled to his feet and limped toward the *barrera*. The crowd jeered. Some stood and yelled, "Come back, coward!" Others cried, "*¡Fuera!* Go home!"

"Why, it's only a surface wound," Rico said. "Where's his pride?"

"I guess he took it with him," I said.

Meanwhile in the bullring, the beast was distracted by the *toreros* with one cape after another. Suddenly, a spectator dropped from the stands onto the arena. He crawled in the sand, then pushed himself up, removed his jacket and dangled it with stiff arms before him. He staggered toward the bull and snarled, "Come here, *toro*!"

"It's Don Ebrio!" I pointed at the drunk and tapped Rico's shoulder.

"Don who?" Eva and Rico chimed.

"You know, the man who fell earlier."

"Are you sure?" Eva squinted.

Rico tossed back his head in a gale of hearty chuckles. "What a comedy! Now the *toreros* have to control an old drunk as well as a bored bull."

El Chico shook his fist at Don Ebrio but remained behind the *barrera*. The crowd whistled and clapped as the old man scurried past the *toreros* and headed for the bull. He tripped and landed in a thud under the beast's snout. The bull sniffed at him, then loped away to stand in the shade.

Groans rumbled around the arena. The president of the bullfight stood and waved a handkerchief to signal the bull unworthy to continue. The *toreros* herded El Flaco Feroz to the arena gate, where he vanished into the dark, gaping exit. Two police officers hastened out, scooped up Don Ebrio and dragged him away. The humiliated matador, El Chico, trudged off, his "suit of lights" now blood-streaked and dusty, his eyes intent on the sand.

Rico shook his head. "They didn't do justice when they chose that bull. The kid grandstanded too much for my taste, *pero* he did manage a smooth little tango with the brute for a while. I hope the next..." Rico waxed on about the virtues of worthy bulls and courageous matadors.

Chapter Eight: La Muerte Meets a Worthy Bull

I hissed behind Rico's back to Eva, "¡Chht!...¡Chht!" Eva turned toward me and shrugged. I patted my stomach and pointed at my open mouth.

"Rico, could we get a snack?" Eva whined.

"Huh?" Rico's rant halted in mid-sentence.

"We're hungry," I piped in.

"*Pues*, I suppose a little something won't hurt, *pero* I don't want you girls to spoil your appetites. We'll have a feast later at the casino. Meanwhile, allow me." He clicked loud castanet fingers in the air. A boy with cinnamon skin and round green eyes appeared, holding a tray of snacks and drinks. Rico took the tray and held it while Eva and I looked at the treats. I chose a tamarind drink and a peanut cluster; Eva, lemonade and a coconut patty. Rico handed the young vendor some coins and waved him away.

The boy stared at the money and grinned. "*Muchas...gracias*," he said and meandered off through the crowd. "Caaahndy...POP...corn, COLD drinks," he sang.

I slurped my drink and nibbled candy as a trumpet blast called everyone's attention to the afternoon's second bullfight. The tremulous microphone coughed the matador's name, "El...El An...gel de...de...La Muerrr...te." The bullfighter was known as the Angel of Death but, then, as if Satan himself grabbed control of the airwaves, an echo rang clear, and only the words "La Muerte" were heard. An awed buzz from spectators swarmed around us because the echo only included the mention of death. Rico seemed unfazed.

"This is a good one," he declared. "Now you'll see a true bullfight, *muchachas*."

The crowd roared to its feet as La Muerte performed a stoic march to the center of the ring. Once there, he stopped, stiffened, arched his back and held his cap straight up, his gaze to the sky. The stands rumbled an expectant roar. The matador rotated full circle, maintained his stance, a human compass, moving only his feet in tiny steps.

"*¡Que viva* La Muerte*! ¡Viva, viva, viva!*" Thunderous cries filled the arena.

La Muerte bent at the waist in a formal bow, straightened, removed his parade cape, swirled it around his body like a huge skirt then dragged it behind him as he paraded toward the *barrera* wall, where he took cover.

"This one's a crowd pleaser!" I announced.

"*Pues*, so far it's just good theatre. Let's see how he does when the bull shares his stage. Here it comes!" Rico said.

Trumpets sounded. The airwaves crackled, "¡El...Gran Fan...tas...ma!"

The massive beast clambered out of the chute and galloped faster than a racehorse to the middle of the ring. Sand sprayed in cloudy trails behind it. The bull wheeled and charged about, tossing its horns. Hoots and whistles reverberated around us.

"A fine bull, this phantom," Rico proclaimed.

"It'll kill the matador," I said.

"Not if he performs well," Rico said.

"One of them will surely die," Eva murmured. Rico chuckled.

I watched La Muerte study the bull from behind the *barrera*. The noise around us dwindled to a fizz of murmurs when the bull slowed to a prance. The matador stepped from behind the *barrera* and paced, head high, toward the brawny beast.

93

The cape-work played like a tango—brilliant, stiff, back-and-forth measured steps, then quick, dramatic twirls—rigid matador and churning beast in a cloud of dust.

"He's already cast a spell on the bull!" Rico praised the matador. "And what a graceful beast he has the privilege of fighting!"

"Soon the poor animal will realize this is no social event. No doubt it'll be dragged out of here," I remarked. Rico nodded.

After a while, the bull seemed to grow dizzy. It swayed its massive bulk against the matador's chest, then stumbled aside, ebony coat lathered in sweat, panting. La Muerte strode toward the stands, trailing the cape behind him, hand on hip, his back to the bull. He held his head high and waved at the stands. Cheers echoed about the arena as he strutted toward the *barrera*.

The splintered corral gates creaked open. Trumpets blared to announce the entrance of the *picadores*. Their horses pranced, some to the right, others to the left of the bull, which stood unfazed in the middle of the arena. The men wore big felt hats, elaborately embroidered bolero jackets and cream-colored buckskin chaps. Each sat tall in the saddle and carried a wooden lance in his right hand while gripping the reins with his left.

One of the horsemen guided his steed toward the bull. El Fantasma pawed at the ground and bounded toward the horse. Although the horse was protected by thick padding, the bull managed to jab its horns into the horse's underbelly, almost overturning horse and rider. In mid-air, the *picador* stabbed at the bull's neck muscles. Another rider approached, distracted the bull and thrust his lance at the furious animal. El Fantasma's mighty horns lifted the horse and tossed the *picador* into the air like a swatted fly. A collective gasp whipped through the air.

The matador sprinted from behind the *barrera* toward the bull. He flapped the satin cape against the animal's snout. El Fantasma responded by bucking and lashing out his hind legs. The bull bounded against the cape and continued away from the intrepid matador, who strutted after it. Meanwhile, several *toreros* helped the stunned *picador* to his feet and led him and his dusty horse away.

El Fantasma galloped wildly, corralling the men in a ring of dust, his domain of terror. The *picador* who'd fallen from his horse stumbled along, glancing from the bull to the stands as a clamor of loud whistles and jeers heightened his humiliation.

"How easily the crowd sours. They think the bull is in control," scoffed Rico, "so they toss their pessimism into the mix. *Pero* keep your eye on the matador. This showdown is between him and El Fantasma."

I glanced at Eva, who powdered her nose, intent on her reflection in a compact mirror. I shoved her shoulder. "Eva, watch La Muerte!" I crossed my eyes at her.

She giggled. "*Prima*, you know I can't watch." She held the mirror closer to her face.

I turned when a resounding "*¡OLÉ!*" swept round the arena. The bullfighter danced in a tight semi-circle before El Fantasma, who appeared hypnotized by the waves of red satin that dangled before him.

"*¡Aja, toro!*" La Muerte commanded, brandishing the cape. The bull swished against the cloth, horns skimming the matador's chest. Then the beast spun back for more, horns searching a solid target. The matador stood still and flicked only his wrist each time El Fantasma glided by, circled back and charged again. The entire arena was in rhythm with the performance, crying "*¡Olé!*" with each flick of the cape.

The matador abruptly lowered the satin distraction alongside the bull. It halted, head bowed, dripping blood and snot, heaving loudly. La Muerte signaled to the president of the bullfight for permission to dismiss the remaining *picadores* and proceed to the next act, the performance of the *banderilleros*. People craned their necks to watch for a response. The president waved a handkerchief to grant the request. Applause rang loud and many of the men jumped to their feet and waved their hats in the air.

The bullfighter motioned away two crestfallen *picadores* who sat hunched in their saddles on the sidelines. They yanked their reins, turned and trotted the horses out through the gate. Some people booed them. Others tossed beer bottles and candy wrappers at them. One of the *picadores* smiled and waved at the crowd.

The matador motioned to the *banderilleros* and stalked toward the *barrera*. Shouts of *"¡Bravo!"* punctuated each step he took.

"Unheard of!" Rico exclaimed. "La Muerte allowed for only one lancing…and a pitiful one at that! The bull has not been weakened enough for the kill. I hope this matador prayed to San Miguel as well as La Virgen this morning."

"Pero the *banderilleros* will help weaken the bull," I ventured.

"Bah! With those *piñata* sticks? They hook just below the hide and only serve to irritate the bull and thrill the audience with all the blood and fury."

A slender young man pranced into the ring, clasping two *banderillas* decorated in bright red and yellow crepe paper. He stopped a few yards from El Fantasma, bent back, knees locked, *banderillas* held high, hook side down, pointed in a V at the bull, which pawed at the sand and snorted.

The *banderillero* charged and El Fantasma lunged toward him. The youth leapt directly over the bull's horns and jabbed the hooks into the lumpy mass behind the head. He leaned into the *banderillas* and used them to leverage away from the menace of sharp horns, then scurried off. His head whipped over his shoulder for a glimpse at the bull. Loud cheers sounded as he strolled to the *barrera* and fetched another pair of *banderillas*. He stood solemn and observed El Fantasma for a while.

The heaving beast pivoted wildly, wagging its head up and down. Then it hurtled from one end of the arena to the other and finally slowed to a trot. The *banderillero* sprinted toward El Fantasma, clicking the colorful sticks together, calling out, "*¡Aja, toro. Aja!*"

The bull halted. The young man shuffled closer, raised the *banderillas* overhead and held the pose. The animal stood its ground.

"*¡Toro!*" The *banderillero* sauntered within a few yards of the bull. The angry beast lunged headlong at the youth, who ran forward and executed a stunning spin over the bull's horns. The *banderillas* wedged into the beast, adorning it with brilliant antenna-like rays that bobbed and flailed about at its every move. Jagged strips of blood shone bright crimson and somber burgundy in the late afternoon sun against El Fantasma's sleek ebony body.

"Good work. This kid knows how to take on a bull. Impressive," Rico mused.

"And he doesn't look scared," I said.

"*Ay, pero* you can be sure that it's his fear that energizes such *machismo*. Either that or a lot of tequila!" Rico slapped his knee and guffawed.

"I think the bull could use some tequila," Eva muttered. "Look at all that blood. *¡Qué horror!*"

"*Ay, tú, tú.* You act like you've never been to a bullfight," I teased.

"Enough, *muchachas*!" Rico said.

As the *banderillero* approached the *barrera*, the matador strode out and raised his cap to the president of the bullfight for approval to move on to the kill. The official quickly waved the handkerchief. Sounds of delight bubbled from the stands. La Muerte looked up, saluted and grinned.

"He's foregoing the last *banderillas*. I think he's afraid that young boy will steal the show," Rico said.

Several *toreros* padded out to distract the bull with some cape-work, while the matador marched around the arena then faced the president's box again. He removed his cap, swooped into a dramatic bow then rose and extended his cap toward the stands.

"I wish to dedicate the death of this worthy bull to the gracious Doña Perfecta!" he proclaimed as he bowed to the president's wife. Gentle applause tapped out polite approval. La Muerte gently tossed his cap toward the fashionably dressed old woman, who soared from her seat and plucked at it, unabashed, then stumbled.

Her husband shot to his feet, steadied his wife with one hand, caught the cap in the other and presented her with it. She held it to her bosom as, in unison, she and her husband donned cardboard smiles and waved stiff arms at the matador and at their audience. The president nodded at La Muerte, who turned on his heel to retrieve the short cape and sword for his final bout with El Fantasma.

The *toreros* continued some flashy cape-work to keep the bull and the masses entertained until the matador returned. The trumpet sounded as he marched solemnly toward the bull, shrill whistles and cheers around him. When he stopped a few yards from the bull, the remaining *toreros* retreated.

The bull wasted no time and charged the matador, whom it now perceived as an adversary and not a dance partner. As the bull shot toward him, La Muerte dropped to his knees and held the cape aside at shoulder level. He swiveled about in the dust when the beast stormed by. A train roar "¡OLÉ!" resonated in sync with the motion of the brute's head tearing past the glitter.

"What a magnificent spin!" Rico yelled. "What a showboat this kid is!"

La Muerte jumped to his feet, now a human maypole, while the bull twisted its agile mass as if to pursue its tail. The *"¡Olés!"* became a constant acoustic blur in rhythm with entangled man and beast, then slowed somewhat with breaks like those in a scratched recording.

"He'll wear us down along with that poor bull if he doesn't get on with it," Rico scoffed.

The rotations on the sand halted suddenly. The bull tossed from side to side in search of the vanished cloth as La Muerte turned away and raised an arm high then crooked it behind the cape. He slid the short sword from behind a fold in the satin. The shiny blade gleamed in the afternoon sun.

The matador held the cape against his groin and the sword behind his back as he shuffled toward El Fantasma. The bull lowered its head at the sight and hesitated. Hushed anticipation filled the air.

"He's asking for trouble!" Rico marveled.

I giggled. "*Ay,* Rico, that's funny. Don't you think so, Eva?"

"Huh?"

"Nothing, silly!"

"What are you saying, Inma? I can't hear you!" Eva yelled.

"Never mind!"

La Muerte approached El Fantasma until they stood only a few feet from each other, both visibly heaving. The bull pawed the ground, then stopped. The matador lunged toward the horns and flew along one side of the bull, stabbing at its shoulders. Blood glimmered in the afternoon sun. El Fantasma scrambled after the matador, unscathed.

La Muerte challenged the fury of the injured beast by swirling the shiny cape about its snout, soon engaging it in back-and-forth runs. When their dance reached a fevered rhythm, the bull began to sway a bit as it charged, outlining bloody figure eights in the sand. Some men waved fists and registered disgust, "Enough, hombre!" and "¡Qué bárbaro!"

"What's this fellow waiting for?" Rico said. "He'll bleed the bull to death."

An angry, persistent chant swelled around us until it reached a deafening crescendo. The matador finally turned on his heel and scampered to the barrera. El Fantasma plunged blindly after him but stopped short when the matador disappeared behind the wooden refuge. A hailstorm of projectiles, from Chiclets and banana peels to empty tequila bottles, raged in the matador's direction.

El Fantasma snorted, pawed at the sand and wagged his horns. The beast turned and galloped to the middle of the arena.

"What a fine bull. He's still strong. The matador waved off help weakening it, *pero* maybe we'll have a good kill yet," Rico said.

"All the blood!" Eva protested. "I can't watch any more of this."

"La Muerte missed the mark, *pero* he can still save face," Rico insisted.

"He doesn't have much face to save!" I laughed.

"And who says you're the expert?" Eva taunted.

"Look around. It'll take some show to bring these people around," I said.

"True," Rico agreed. "The crowd shamed the matador and took control. *Pero* everyone underestimated the bull's power for all the blood. This may still prove a fair match. An injured bull. A disgraced matador. Fickle spectators." He looked at me.

I nodded and grinned.

"After all," Rico continued, "the bull has shown it can still fight. If La Muerte delivers an honorable kill, he'll force cheers from these cynics. Just watch!" Rico jutted his jaw toward the matador, who emerged from his retreat to face both beast and crowd.

"Don't back down!" *"¡No te rajes!"* someone bellowed as the matador stomped toward El Fantasma. But most people chose not to further razz the matador and watched as he captured the bull's attention at great distance by flapping a circular taunt with the cape. With arm outstretched at shoulder level, he flicked a skillful wrist, entrancing both beast and onlookers with twirls of glittering cape and camouflaged sword. Anticipation softly settled where frustration had lingered.

A single *"¡Aja, toro!"* rang out across the quiet arena as man and bull paced toward each other. When the matador stopped, El Fantasma followed his lead. The bull stared at a now-still cape. Spectators leaned forward at the gleam of the short sword—the one used for the kill. La Muerte studied the bull's stance.

"He's going in!" Rico whispered.

"Sí, qué bueno." I forced a grin and glanced at Eva, who sat bolt upright, hands over her eyes.

La Muerte shuffled until he stood within feet of the bull's widespread horns. Everyone stilled when he released the cape and it drifted, ebbing and flowing in a mesmerizing glide to the ground. El Fantasma's head dropped, eyes on the cloth. La Muerte tapped his sword between the beast's shoulder blades, turned on his heel, waltzed away and abandoned the cape, which diverted the bull and drove most people to their feet. Clamorous shouts of *"¡Bravo!"* ran up and down the bleachers, as the matador stood motionless before mob and beast.

The matador swiveled about, blade angled, and pranced, legs stiff before him, toward his mark. He shifted to a slow gait as he neared the bull, which nudged about, wrestling the limp cape on the ground.

Calm signaled a quiet invitation. *"Eh, toro...Aja."* Heels together, toes pointed outward, La Muerte inched his satin slippers through bloody dust, sword overhead. El Fantasma jerked up, snorted and glared at the unwelcomed commotion. The matador's eyes remained fixed on the spot his sword must penetrate to bring a quick death for the bull and a graceful end to his own performance. Not a sound from onlookers. Vendors stopped their hawking and froze in the aisles. Fistfuls of popcorn and peanuts hovered before open mouths. Babies quit crying. Birds flapped silent wings.

La Muerte stomped his foot. The bull lowered its head, spreading open its vulnerable point. The matador quickly thrust his weapon so deep that only the handle remained visible. The mighty beast dropped to its knees, rolled aside and lay at rest. For a long moment everyone in the arena remained still as they gawked at the scene before them. The crowd seemed to take a collective deep breath as if in disbelief.

Then resounding roars of *"¡BRAVO!"* assaulted my ears. Thunderous stomping vibrated through my body and shook my lungs. The band broke into an animated celebration for the honorable death of the worthy bull.

"Is it over?" Eva whined, her hands still over her eyes.

"Yes, you silly goose!" I answered.

Many people waved handkerchiefs requesting La Muerte be granted the coveted trophy for his performance—one of the bull's ears. The matador pasted a wide-toothed smile across his face and waved at well-wishers until he caught glimpse of the president signaling the end of the bullfight. La Muerte's teeth vanished behind a tight-lipped grin as he bowed slightly then marched out of the arena. Several *toreros* hustled toward the dead bull, hoisted it onto a horse-drawn wooden pallet and dragged away its remains. Polite applause marked the departure of both man and beast.

"*Pues*, that ended well," Rico said. "He didn't get the cut ear, *pero* he regained control of the show. You've got to grant him that."

"He did just fine," Eva chirped.

"You saw very little of it," I chided.

"More than enough!" she insisted.

"Maybe they should present this bull the matador's ear." I laughed.

"*Ay qué muchacha.* That bull is being filleted for dinner even as we speak," Rico quipped.

"Not ours, I hope."

"What's that?" Rico said.

"No, nothing, Rico," I replied.

"I heard what you said." Eva grinned at me and giggled.

"Never mind all that. Do you want to go freshen up?" I leaned my head aside.

"*Sí, buen idea.* Rico, please excuse us. We want to go freshen up."

Rico stood. "Let me come with you. I don't want you to walk through this mob unescorted."

"*Pero,* could we go to my house to freshen up, *por favor?*" I hesitated when Rico's brows crumpled together. "It's just down the road," I continued. "You know, the facilities here are less than adequate." I pinched an up-turned nose.

Rico chuckled. "Of course, I'll have the driver take you. Wait here."

I lifted a shoulder and blinked respect. He craned his neck in search of the driver. "And don't be long. El Victor is next," Rico said.

Chapter Nine: Casting Spells and Brujerías

We waited for swirls of dust to settle before stepping out of the car. Eva and I emerged, one at a time, guided by the driver's extended hand. Neighbors stopped their afternoon gossip, mouths agape, rocking chairs motionless, and set down their cardboard fans. Several boys screeched their bicycles to full stop, straddled them, and maneuvered stiff-legged and barefooted across the dirt for a closer look at the huge, late model Ford. Two small girls hurried by, whispered behind cupped hands and giggled away.

"Why are they laughing?" I muttered.

"Never mind. Let's hurry," Eva said.

We entered the house through the store, where Doña Inez anguished over a piece of paper in her hand. "I can't read this scrawling. What a witch this fortune teller is. She writes on a greasy snip of butcher paper." Her head jerked aside when she heard us walk in. Her eyes narrowed at us, piercing a trail from our fancy hairdos and flounced crepe down to the points of our satin shoes.

"Mamá, we'll just be a few minutes," I announced. My mother responded with a look toward the old woman.

"*Ah, sí, buenas tardes*, Doña Inez." A strained grin wrestled the groan from my sing-song greeting. Eva twinkled demure.

"*Ay, muchachas*, God's Angels of Mercy bring you in my hour of need!" the old woman huffed, her ragged eyebrows twitching up and down.

I puffed a brazen sigh and pouted at Mamá. She shook her head.

"*Pero*, Doña Inez, they know nothing about such things," Mamá soothed. Her eyes darted a blessing for us to take flight. I focused on the door.

"*¡No, no!* You must help me." The old woman grabbed my hand and clutched it to her bosom. I froze as she teetered on the balls of her feet.

"*Por favor*, Doña Inez! What is it?" I punctuated my disrespect with a scowl.

"*Hija*, don't speak to her like that." Mamá frowned.

111

"*No, no*, she has every right. I must sound like *una loca. Pero, por favor*, two minutes," the tiny woman pleaded.

"¡Mamááá!" I whined.

Eva patted my shoulder and stepped forward. "How can we help?" she asked.

I tapped my foot and meditated on a can of peas behind the counter.

"*Pues,* you know, the fortune teller, that witch, treated me for nerves, *pero* it didn't help. And then, *pues*, she, you know, the fortune teller, that witch, she read my cards again and again, *y pues*, you see, she, the fortune teller, that *bruja*, she insists something horrible will happen today." Doña Inez paused, saucer-eyed. "Unless…*pues*, she says, *la bruja* says, I must do all this before the moon rises." She opened a trembling hand and the crinkled paper flipped onto the counter.

"You see? She's cast a spell on it and scribbled wicked letters no one can read." She clutched gnarled fingers to her face.

"Doña Inez, *por favor*. Is this curse meant for you?" I said flatly.

112

"*Pues*, she didn't say."

"Then ignore her," I urged. "Rip this up and destroy her power over you." I struggled to suppress exasperation and reached for the note.

"*¡No, no!* I must do what it says!" She grabbed my hand. "My cards delivered the warning." Doña Inez twisted her head from side to side. "*Ay, por favor*, help me read it." She jutted a quivering jaw at the greasy note and shrugged. "That's all I ask."

"*Pues*, let's just see." I scooped up the note, squinted at it and muttered, "Ah, these are symbols, not letters. Eva, look." I tilted my head, handed her the paper and grinned.

She nodded, scrunched her nose and focused. "You're right, *pero*, I can't make out what it means. Can you?" she taunted.

I snatched the note away and held it to my face. "Uh…it says you must light a candle to San Alejo, then, uh, recite fifty Hail Marys."

"Fifty Hail Marys! Such a penance is fit only for the sins of El Diablo himself." The old woman rocked back and forth, hugging herself tight. "Go on, *mija*," she pleaded.

I shot a sideways glance at Mamá. She mouthed a no. I feigned nonchalance. "That is all it says, Doña."

"Are you sure?" the old woman accused.

"*Ah, sí*, I forgot. You must pray by the light of the moon."

"*Pero,* the fortune teller, she said I must complete this before nightfall."

My stomach fluttered. "*Sí, pero*, I think what she meant was, uh…" I heard Eva cough a weak attempt to camouflage a giggle. She mumbled something and shuffled out of the store.

For a moment, I escaped by staring into a picture calendar on the wall. A mustachioed mariachi on horseback tipped his sombrero to a buxom girl with long black braids. She stood in a storybook meadow confettied with flowers and scampering chickens. A farmhouse framed by puffy trees and layers of sunset stood in the horizon.

Somehow, an idea tumbled from my trance. "Uh, you must be home before sunset, Doña. Then you must pray facing the light of the moon."

Her brows flared high, rippling her leathery skin to the hairline. "*Ah, sí,* first I get the candle. And what else?"

I whooshed. "*Pues,* put an aloe vera plant at your door, turn all your holy cards upside down, and drink two cups of linden tea for your nerves," I chanted, mesmerized by Mamá's facial contortions after each of my pronouncements.

"*¡Ayyy, gracias a Dios Santísimo!*" Doña Inez shook stiff arms, palms to the ceiling and tossed back her head. "I can surely do all that!"

"Good luck," I mumbled. "*Buena suerte.*"

"*Ay, muchas gracias, mija. Gracias, Señora,*" she said to Mamá. "You have saved my life." She hurried to the doorway. "I must get to the herb store before they close." She flapped her hands in farewell and disappeared.

"That bothersome old *vieja,*" I muttered.

"¡María Inmaculada!" Mamá's tone startled me. "I would like to know just where you learned such witchcraft, such *brujerías?*"

I shrugged. "I just read what it said."

"What shame! You dare try to fool your own mamá?"

"No, no, of course not," I whined an apology and ventured, "*pero*, you saw how terrified she was. I had to come up with something." I shifted away from her frown.

"Who told you about San Alejo?"

"I'm late, Mamá." I scratched a foot against the floor and whimpered my ultimate plea for salvation: "I need to pee."

"Answer my question."

"*Bueno*. I didn't want to tell you, *pero* remember the séance you and those ladies had after Papá died? That's where I learned it!"

"*¡Ave María Purísima!*" Mamá raised praying hands to her mouth.

"I swear, it was an accident. As I walked back from Eva's that night, I saw candlelight through the window. The shutters were open so I couldn't help but hear everything. I peeked under the curtains to watch that gypsy woman."

"*Ay, mija*, I wish you'd told me." Mamá's eyes hazed. "Now you've given advice you know nothing about to a desperate woman," she murmured.

"*Pues*, I had to do something. I only did it because I felt quite desperate myself. Mamá, *por favor,* I won't have time to look in a mirror if I don't hurry! I'll miss the bullfight. El Victor!" I whined.

Mamá shrugged. "*Bueno pues*, I suppose we can discuss this later. You may hurry along."

*   *   *

"What are you upset about?" Eva beaded her eyes at me as we bumped along in Rico's car on our return to the bullring.

"What else? That old *loca* stole all my time! Not to mention you abandoned me."

"I had to. It was either that or giggle in her face."

"How could you laugh at a time like that?"

"*Oye*, what's really the matter? You've pouted all afternoon." Eva's tone softened.

"Nothing...*ay, pues*, maybe I do envy all the attention you get. Even that *banderillero* turned into a statue at the sight of you. Then you get to doll yourself up while I barely have time to...*ay*, never mind. I don't care. Besides, you'll probably get the evil eye!"

"*Ah, pero* which one will it be?" Eva blinked crossed eyes at me.

"Pfft!" My resentment gave way to guffaws.

"Do I look better like this?" She rolled open her bottom lip.

"Eva, you're as loony as Doña Inez!"

"Better. I got you to laugh, Inma."

"First time today. Rico so serious about the bullfight, and every time I look over, you're staring at yourself in the mirror."

"I can't help it. I don't like to watch the violence. The first part is okay. You know, when the matador seduces the bull into a ballet."

"A ballet? More like a tango."

"You mean a tangle. After while, you can't see the bull for the cape."

"Who cares about bulls?" I said. "I watch the matadors. Just think, El Victor is here. He'll look great prancing about in those tight pants."

"*Oye, tú*, what have you done with my innocent young cousin?" Eva chuckled.

"She's gone mad for the biggest star to ever grace this town, is what. And now we've missed most of the bullfight." I pretended to swoon, hand to forehead.

"Wonder if he'll be at the *tardeada*?" Eva said.

"Of course he will...he'd better be." I tugged at the sticky flower in my hair.

"Don't get hysterical, Doña Pánico. Remember, the matador who got gored? I think he had his eye on you." Eva smiled. "I'm certain *he'll* be there."

"*Sí*, and so will your statue!"

Chapter Ten: Victor Victorious, "¡Olé, Olé, Olé!"

The driver escorted us back to our seats. Rico stood and waved as we approached. "Hurry, *muchachas.*" He moved aside as Eva and I took our places next to him. "You've missed most of the bullfight," he muttered.

"I knew it!" I exclaimed.

"Is everything all right?" Rico's eyebrows arched. Eva and I bobbed our heads and looked toward the arena.

El Victor glittered in the late afternoon sun, a white "suit of lights" snug against his muscular body. His sun-kissed hair and tanned face complemented his youthful looks. Shoulders back, head high, he padded around the perimeter, waving at the boisterous crowd while some *toreros* kept the bull bounding after their capes.

"He's more handsome in person!" I whispered to Eva. She nodded with lifted brows.

"He's magnificent!" Rico sniffed. "Smooth, classic moves. You'll see. He's been granted the go-ahead for the kill. And the bull has lived up to its name, El Vencedor, a conqueror. Strong like an ox, *pero* graceful as a swan."

I glanced toward the bull and gasped. "*Dios mío,* it's huge." El Vencedor bucked and pranced in jagged circles, while the colorful *banderilla* skewers stuck in his body waved akimbo at every bounce.

"A bull worthy of nothing less than a perfect kill," Rico said.

As El Victor passed us, he hesitated and gleaned a perfect white smile. His march around the arena afforded him an eye-level glance at spectators in the box seats.

"He's looking at you!" Eva pinched my elbow.

"Is not!" I folded arms to chest but trembled a tiny grin. "His eyes are on you," I insisted. Nevertheless, I grinned as the famous matador strode off.

"I'm sure he found you both beautiful," Rico chided.

The matador advanced to the president's box. On the opposite end of the arena, several *toreros* scampered about like boys in a soccer game, vying for attention from both the bull and spectators.

El Victor curved in a formal bow to the president then walked toward us. The crowd roared. Trumpets blared.

"He's coming back!" I said.

"Cupid's arrow has struck! I told you he liked you," Eva chirruped.

"*Ay, por favor*. Quit it." I shoved her.

The handsome young matador halted before our box and swept into a full bow. The arena grew quiet. I squeezed Eva's wrist tight.

"Ouch!" She hissed through a decorous smile and dug a fingernail into my arm.

Rico said, "I think he's going to dedicate the bull to one of you. *Pero*, I don't know which one."

"We'll see. He can't throw the cap to both of us." I nodded and smiled at the young matador.

Rico chuckled approval and murmured, "He's clever, this one."

El Victor announced, "I wish to dedicate the death of this noble bull to the beauty of the women of México!" He stepped back and, with a gentle underhand toss, launched his cap in our direction. It arched toward Rico, who plucked it from the air directly under his nose. The matador hesitated.

"Ah, he's tricky, all right. Here, *muchachas*, take the cap and hold it up together."

"Maybe he likes Rico!" I giggled to Eva.

"Stand up, *muchachas*! Everyone must see you. Turn around, turn...now wave!" Rico commanded. Loud applause erupted.

"Now we're sure to get the evil eye," I said. "Everyone's staring."

"Yes, with plenty of envy, I'm sure. Smile, *prima*," Eva said.

"*Bueno*, now face El Victor and bow, no, curtsy, no...here, hand me the cap... just wave. You know, like you're slicing the air. Like this." Rico stood and demonstrated.

"We look like marionettes in a chorus line!" Eva chuckled.

The matador waved back then marched to the *barrera,* where a young boy handed him the small cape and short sword for the kill. The band bleated a shaky tune as the matador pranced toward the bull. The *toreros* around the bull flitted away, flashing cape swirls on their way to the *barrera.*

"Which of you wants El Victor's cap?" Rico smiled.

"Keep it." Eva took the cap from Rico and handed it to me. "He meant it for you!"

"Did not!" I shoved it away. "You're the one he yearns for." I giggled.

"Let me have that!" Rico said. He took the cap, stared at it and traced the gold embroidery with his fingers.

"You should keep it, Rico," I said. "After all, you caught it."

"Perhaps I will. You girls will surely have an entire collection of these before long," he purred.

"Eva will, not me," I said.

"You really think so, Inma?" Eva blushed.

"*Ay, muchachas,* for now, let's enjoy this matador's little game."

"You mean the bullfight?" I asked.

"No, I mean his schemes for tonight."

I shrugged at Eva. She leaned close, crossed her eyes and hovered a cuckoo signal next to her ear. "You're hopeless." I sighed.

El Victor paced toward the bull, cape waist high before him. He fluttered a taunt at El Vencedor with each step. The bull snorted and pawed at the ground. Man and beast, like familiar dance partners, flowed into a series of classic swirls and full-circled *veronicas.*

"*Muchachas,* you are in the presence of greatness! Here's traditional cape-work. Nothing fancy. No tricks." Rico glanced at us.

"And he's so tall," said Eva.

I sighed. "I wonder what color his eyes are? They looked green to me." I leaned and squinted toward the bullfighter.

"You are too much, Inma." Eva rolled her eyes and giggled.

Soon the entire arena seemed to pulsate in rhythm. A symphony of *"¡Olés!"* celebrated the choreography in the sand. Garish satin flashes, stoic man and bloodied, undaunted beast waltzed together, breezed apart. Cheers, whistles, and cries of *"¡Ajúa!"* sounded in a tempo that grew faster and louder, mounting to a climax. The matador rotated to *"¡olé!"*, sauntered, spun, *"¡Olé!"*, strutted, whirled, *"¡OLÉ!"*, reeled, reeled, and reeled again, *"¡OLÉ, OLÉ, OLÉ!"*

El Victor abruptly stepped aside from the bull's charge, stalked away and saluted onlookers. Sombreros, *sarapes* and popcorn flew into the air. Everyone on their feet. Thunderous applause, shrieks and *gritos* followed. Infants spilled from parents' laps. Would-be matadors tumbled into the arena and lunged toward the bull, only to be tackled by awaiting *toreros*. The mighty beast, El Vencedor, stood firm, eyes steady on the cape.

Trumpets sounded. Drums rolled. El Victor pulled the sword from its sleeve in one deft move, clasped his fingers over its handle and positioned it under the cape. Quiet respect filled the air. El Victor about-faced, marched toward the bull and invited it to

126

dance with a flick of the cape. The beast studied the cloth, while El Victor padded closer. Suddenly, the bull sprang forward and El Victor jumped aside. The beast's horns followed the satin cape that soon snapped over its head. The bull sashayed round El Victor. Several hushed *"¡olés!"* broke the silence in the stands. El Victor turned to face the bull.

The dance in the sand continued, proving the beast yet strong, graceful and trusting. Blood decorated it in ragged strips below the *banderillas*. Its charge remained lively, seemingly unscathed by its partner's treason.

After a few more twirls, El Victor sidestepped away from the bull, spun round, moved the cape into the opposite hand and met the charge with his back to the bull. The crowd roared. The bull circled back, faced the matador, then halted, bobbed its head and snorted. It gazed side to side. El Victor gripped the cape, arched his back, hips forward, shoulders back and padded toward the bull.

"He's ready for the kill!" Rico rubbed his hands together.

"I can't look! I can't look!" Eva held her fan over her face.

"Don't worry, I'll tell you all about it later." I pushed the fan into her nose.

"¡Chhht, silencio, por favor, muchachas!" Rico shook his head.

El Victor moved about, his posterior to the bull and eyed the beast over his shoulder. El Vencedor grunted, pawed at the dust, flared his nostrils and held his ground, head bowed. The matador shifted about in the sand, faced the bull, fluttered the cape toward the left and grasped the blade in his right hand. He wiggled the satin against his thighs and raised the sword at an angle toward his opponent. The bull lowered its gaze then sprinted, horns first, toward the cape.

El Victor scurried forward and yanked the cape aside an instant before he stood on tiptoes and leaned over the bull, driving the sword deep between its shoulder blades. The young matador then high-stepped away from El Vencedor. A collective gasp stilled the air as the huge beast dropped to its knees, fell sideways into the sand and stiffened, eyes wide.

The crowd roared to its feet. The band bellowed a spirited "ta-ta-ra-ta...tar-ra-ra-ta" victory tune. El Victor bowed before the officials' box while several *toreros* rushed to the bull, then nodded to the president. He looked around the arena, which had exploded in flickering handkerchiefs, a signal of approval from spectators. The president signaled that both the bull's ears be cut. The arena thundered approval.

"A perfect kill!" Rico said. "El Victor is…"

The noise muffled the rest of Rico's comments. Spectators bid farewell to the proud bull with a round of applause as the *toreros* dragged it away on a horse-drawn wooden pallet.

"I can't hear you!" I yelled at Rico, who waved his hands in the air. Foot-stomping, shouting, whistling and tinny squawks from the trumpet seemed to swallow and shake the stands.

He leaned closer. "Best bullfight I've ever seen!"

I dizzied amidst the crowd, an ocean that pulsated with white handkerchiefs, wide-brimmed sombreros and human arms. Several *toreros* sprinted toward El Victor, hoisted him over their shoulders and paraded him around the arena. Men and boys of all ages popped onto the bullring and crushed around the bullfighter. Hundreds of roses and carnations floated a lush mantle over bloody sand and sweaty men, who carried El Victor out the arena gate, into the village.

"*Vámonos, muchachas.*" Rico tapped my shoulder, stood and motioned to the driver.

Eva and I scrambled to our feet. We trailed the driver and dodged elbows, sombreros and parasols toward the exit.

As the driver helped us into the car, the *macho* parade chanted by, *"¡Que viva El Victor! ¡Que viva!"* The matador's gaze followed us as he bobbled by, flaunting a toothy façade of glee for his public.

Soon we rumbled off, away from the commotion. Rico turned in his seat to face us and smiled. "It's very obvious El Victor likes you girls. I'm just not sure which one of you he likes most. We shall see."

Chapter Eleven: Afternoon Envy and Grace

"We're early!" I said as we walked into the near-empty casino.

One of the waiters hurried toward us. *"Bienvenidos, Señor, Señoritas."*

"Buenas tardes, Manuel. Everything ready?" Rico scanned the scene.

"Sí, Señor." Manuel flung a stiff arm in the direction of several waiters who hovered next to a table by the dance floor. They snapped fresh linens, arranged silverware and placed crystal goblets next to several bottles of cognac.

Rico nodded. "The girls will have mineral water," he said as we started toward our table. Manuel's eyes darted aside, and one waiter whisked bottles to the center of the table. Another scurried toward the bar and returned, bucket of ice and drinks in hand. Manuel screeched back my chair while Rico did the same for Eva.

After I was seated, she leaned toward me. "You led with it!"

"I what?"

"You leaned into your chair! Don't you remember what Doña Alta Sociedad said? How a proper lady should lower straight into a chair, not stick her backside toward it first. You led with your derrière, *muchacha*. I think one of the waiters fell in love." She glanced at Manuel, statue-stoic at Rico's side.

"You better hush!" I hissed through a forced grin. I turned away from her and smiled at Rico as he took his place.

The waiters opened bottles, clinked ice, poured drinks and waited, grins plastered well in place. Rico mumbled something over his shoulder to Manuel who, with the lift of an eyebrow, sent the waiters shuffling off.

I reached for my drink. Eva grabbed my wrist and nodded in Rico's direction.

He raised a cognac-filled snifter. "*Salud, muchachas*."

"*Salud*." I slurped the mineral water down to the ice and turned to Eva. "Let's go powder our noses."

She nodded mid-sip and set down her drink. "*Con permiso*, Rico."

His chair moaned against the floor as he rose to his feet and bowed slightly.

"*Pasen, muchachas.*"

We gathered our evening bags and teetered away. Lola's heels were a size too big on me, and the cotton I'd stuffed in the toe of one shoe had disappeared. "I'm afraid I'll lead with my rear end again, *prima*!" I pointed at the shoes. "Only this time, I'll land on the floor."

"Walk on your tiptoes!" Eva whispered. "And keep your legs stiff. Like this." She stalked ahead.

"Like a ballerina on stilts? Next time, I wear my own shoes!" I wobbled past her, clawed at the bathroom door and swung it open.

Inside, two girls, busy at the mirror, applied lipstick, fussed with hairdos and continued their chatter, oblivious to our arrival. They wore beautiful evening dresses: one, a shiny taffeta, the other, a soft silk. It was obvious that, unlike us, these girls had changed dresses after the bullfight. I sighed and gawked at them.

One of the girls waved her hands in the air as she spoke. "She's running away with him tonight. Bertita's mother found out that the hussy fortune teller even hoodwinked his wife out of all her money. And if you ask me, he's no prize. Have you seen him? That pockmarked old hunchback! Can you imagine kissing a man that ugly?"

"*Ay, no*, I'd rather lick a frog!" The other girl stuck out her tongue and wiggled it.

Their laughter ricocheted against the walls. I crossed my eyes at Eva, sidled closer to the mirror and tilted my head for her to follow suit.

"You mean Doña Inez, don't you?" I directed my question to one girl's reflection in the mirror. She said nothing. "Her husband is running away with the fortune teller?" I repeated to her in the mirror.

The girl turned to look at me. I hadn't recognized her. She was Cristina Chávez, the queen of La Cosecha's fair. She was affectionately nicknamed "La Chiquis" by everyone who knew her.

"Pardon me," she said softly, "I didn't realize you were speaking to me." She looked at Eva and me. "Forgive our loud gossip. I'm sure you couldn't help but overhear."

134

I blushed. "Aren't you La Chiquis?" I stammered.

"That's what everyone calls me." She smiled. "*Pero* how rude of me. Let me introduce my friend and myself. This is Valeria and I'm Cristina."

"*Mucho gusto,*" Eva and I gushed.

"And I recognize you two young beauties from the bullfight. We're so envious, aren't we, Valeria? El Victor tossed you his cap, didn't he?" She bared perfect teeth in a wide smile.

"He did!" I said proudly.

"*Pero*, we're at a disadvantage here, *muchachas*, because we don't know your names," she continued, ever so slyly.

"I'm Inma and this is my cousin Eva. We're pleased to meet you." I nodded.

"You're not members here, are you? Aren't you a little young to be at the socials?" Valeria asked abruptly. I blinked at her.

"Now, Valeria, stop that!" La Chiquis admonished. "Is that any way to treat our new friends?" She smiled at us.

"All I meant is that I don't recognize them from the casino, that's all," Valeria replied.

"No, we're not members. We're guests of Rico de la Lana," I said proudly.

"Of course, we all know Rico. He's such a delightful character, isn't he, girls?" La Chiquis grinned.

Eva and I nodded. Valeria said, "You mean Don Rico of La Sembradora? Everyone knows him." She rolled her eyes.

"There. That's something we can all agree on. You girls have a lovely evening. We've got to get back," La Chiquis said in a hushed, soothing tone. "Nice to have met you." She smiled over her shoulder. "Valeria, are you coming, dear?"

Not a word to us from Valeria as she followed La Chiquis out the door.

"They are so beautiful," I said to Eva. "Aren't they?"

"Sure, but we got the cap!" She giggled.

I suddenly remembered that La Chiquis never answered my question about Doña Inez. "Hey, she never revealed who was betrayed by the fortune teller!" I said to Eva.

"Who cares? Everyone gets betrayed by that witch!" she retorted.

"You know what I think?" I said. "Those high society girls like La Chiquis don't ever spread gossip. We caught her gossiping and she gracefully got out of revealing anything."

"No, instead she charmed you half to death! I swear, Inma. You were star struck!"

"You've got to admit she is beautiful. And what manners!"

"Forget about Her Royal Highness! Here, help me touch up my hair." Eva handed me a comb.

I turned to look in the mirror. "Yours? Look at mine! I look like I fell off a burro. Why didn't you tell me I looked so bad?"

"Here, have some wine," Eva purred.

"Where on earth did you get that?"

"One of those smart alecks must have left it behind."

"Why do you call them smart alecks?" I asked.

"You're so naïve, *prima*! It's because they know how to insult and condescend with such charm. They're experts!"

I shrugged. "I guess you're right, Eva." I squinted at my reflection. "*Madre Santísima*, I'm a fright." Perspiration had bumped beads of makeup across my forehead and down my shiny nose.

"Look at this mess!" Eva pointed. Her hair lay in damp clumps, sticky from excessive doses of La Cleopatra's hair spray.

"Pfft!" I stifled a giggle too late.

"What are you laughing at, Cactus Head?" Eva smirked at me in the mirror.

I groaned at the sight—hair in spikes that dangled bobby pins like so many clothespins on taut lines. "Wish I had a hat."

"Quit grumbling and start brushing." Eva yanked a hairbrush out of my bag.

*　　　　*　　　　*

"You're glamorous!" Rico stood as we approached the table. "Love the look! Sleek-haired brunettes. Like movie stars. ¡*Muy guapas*!" He yanked chairs for us and pointed. "I hope you're ready for some appetizers."

"*Ay*, Rico. You shouldn't have waited." Eva stared at the seafood cocktails.

"Nonsense. I've enjoyed the company of my friend." He swirled his cognac and chuckled.

I gazed into the huge glass goblet before me, where a potpourri of murky ingredients floated in red *salsa*. Oysters and shrimp, I recognized, but what about those stringy gray things? I looked at Eva, who zigzagged a spoon over her serving, glanced at me and wrinkled her nose.

"*¡Buen provecho, muchachas!*" Rico hoisted his drink. "I've ordered our dinner!"

I floated my napkin to the floor, tilted aside to pick it up and whispered, "Yuck!"

Eva raised her napkin to cover a giggle, and a pulpy red mess plopped onto the table.

I whisked my napkin off the floor and curled it over Eva's spill. Her eyes danced mischief from me to Rico, who slurped cognac after each bite, oblivious.

"Mmm. *¡Qué delicioso! Pero*, you've hardly touched yours, Eva," he said. She shook her head at me, turned to Rico, now busy scooping out the last of his shrimp.

I thrashed out an arm to pinch her, swatted a goblet instead and blanched when the seafood goo spurted through the air and splattered Rico's face with what looked like a bad rash. Some of the mess sprawled around the liquor bottles and crept in rivulets toward the edge of the table.

Eva bolted upright and knocked over her chair. Rico dabbed at his face and gawked, jaws wide, as a tiny waterfall of the stuff dripped onto his lap. I grabbed my napkin and tried to stop more of the red that threatened Rico's trousers. Several waiters rushed up, gathered bottles, crystal and goblets, then clutched tablecloth ends together and scurried off, clinking silverware in a linen *maraca*.

"I'm sorry." I shook my head at Rico. "It was an accident."

"She didn't mean to." Eva shrugged.

"Of course not." Rico whisked a hand across his pants. His eyes rounded when the spots spread across his groin. He moaned, red-faced, *"Con permiso, muchachas,"* and disappeared.

It's all your fault!" I hissed at Eva.

"Me? You're the clumsy one. Anyhow, just think, now we won't have to eat it." She unfurled a sly grin.

"Pfft!" I burst into a giggle fit. Eva and I were still laughing when two waitresses arrived with fresh table linens.

One of them grimaced, snapped the tablecloth in place and mumbled something to the other, who stood by and nodded, bottom lip curled, napkins clutched in her fists.

"I agree with you." Eva glanced toward the waitresses.

"What did you want?" One of the waitresses asked as she smoothed the tablecloth.

"I'm sorry, did you say something?" Eva asked.

"I thought you wanted something else," she said, frowning.

"No, I was just agreeing with my very wise *prima*," Eva nodded at me, "that some things are better left unsaid."

"Especially gossip!" I sniffed.

"Pardon me," the waitress responded. She stood by and tapped her foot while the other girl set the table.

"Think nothing of it, dear." Eva smiled wide.

I noticed that one of the waitresses rolled her eyes as the two stalked off, just as Manuel escorted other guests to the next table.

"Back to the kitchen, *muchachas*!" He clapped his hands at them.

"How quickly you learned from La Chiquis, Eva," I said.

She giggled. "You did fine yourself. It's fun being a 'real lady', isn't it?"

"Ah, but you win the grand prize." I laughed.

Eva's smile vanished. "Quick, take a seat. Rico's headed this way with Lola and her Don Juan boyfriend. Looks like Rico found some clean trousers somewhere."

We sat and watched them cross the dance floor while the casino rippled alive. People threaded their animation throughout the ballroom, babbling enthusiasm, shuffling shoes, clinking heels, whooshing fabric, fluttering evening bags. Perfumes battled for attention as each person floated by, nodded, head high, confidence affixed in a pageant of designs—from garish and gauche to chic. Chairs groaned, liquor gurgled, chatter surged, laughter gushed, back-slaps cracked in the air. The orchestra musicians tuned their instruments, with a trembling calliope of twangs, strums, and squawks. The bandleader tested microphones in a litany of taps and screeches.

"Look who's here, *muchachas*! Doesn't your sister look stunning, Eva? You've met Juan de Dios of course." Rico's eyes darted mirth.

Eva and I stared. Juan de Dios grinned, leaned aside and grabbed at a chair to steady himself. Lola blushed and shook her head. "We're not sitting here, Juan."

"Huh?" Lola's boyfriend looked startled.

"Of course you are." Rico signaled for them to take a seat.

"*Gracias, pero* Juan's sister is waiting for us," Lola replied, her eyes fixed on her wobbly date. "You girls look very nice," she monotoned.

"So do you," Eva said.

"I especially like your shoes and evening bags." Lola sniffed, eyebrows raised.

"What, these old things?" Eva grinned.

Lola scowled. "Never mind all that. Let's go, Juan." She took him by the arm and they staggered off. "*Gracias*, Rico," she called over her shoulder.

"Quite a character, that fellow of hers," Rico mused.

"*Puro borracho* is what! A drunk!" I said.

"My poor sister." Eva giggled. "She'll have to prop him up all night."

"I'm surprised at Lola," Rico said. Then he looked over my head. "Ah, here's our dinner."

144

The waitress furrowed her brow as she traipsed around the table, ladling portions of a chicken rice casserole, *arroz con pollo,* into bowls and placing one at each setting. As she positioned mine, I studied her face. Tiny wart-like moles freckled her face and changed shape with each expression. When she reached Rico, her face smoothed, a semblance of bland civility, and some of the moles seemed to flatten. As she approached Eva, her face tightened, and they appeared to bead up, little boogers at attention. When she caught me staring, she gave me a look so bold, I turned away. When I glanced back, she had vanished into the din of activity.

Waiters buzzed back and forth from the kitchen to the tables, trays hoisted stiff-armed overhead. Volume levels of gossip, wit and teasing among diners, lulled to a simmer, punctuated by intermittent peals of laughter that seemed to ping-pong in a strategic course between tables set yards apart. A cloud of smoke rose over the bar, where men huddled close, slapped each other's backs and took turns toasting and telling jokes, celebrating their *machismo.*

"This is delicious!" I scooped some of the casserole onto a slice of French bread.

"Very good." Eva nodded.

"The waiter recommended it." Rico smirked at me. "I know your mother doesn't like pork, so I ordered chicken instead."

"*Ay, no,* Mamá doesn't mind. It's just that I got sick once from eating too many *tamales*. So I always..."

An abrupt stillness came over the ballroom. We turned to see what the quiet was about. Manuel escorted El Victor and some of the other matadors across the dance floor. The sounds in the room grew heavy with hums of approval. Someone at the bar yelled, *"¡Ajúa!"* Applause exploded around the room. The celebrated matador bowed slightly and smoothed his hair with one hand. He appeared taller and more debonair than he had in the bullring.

Manuel hesitated while his most prestigious guest of the evening recognized the audience. The celebrated matador and his entourage followed Manuel to a table next to ours. The floor yielded a chorus of noises as the men tugged chairs and took their places.

"*Ay, muchachas,* he's looking over here." Rico returned the bullfighter's smile and nodded.

I followed Rico's gaze and squinted. El Victor's eyes remained locked on the back of Eva's head.

As if she sensed a pat on the shoulder, Eva turned and met the matador's stare. The corners of her mouth trembled into a tiny, coy grin when he nodded.

146

Suddenly, El Victor puckered up his face, tapped a forefinger in the air and pointed at Eva's back. Rico and I leaned behind Eva and strained to see what the famous man might be pointing at. A veil of peas, rice and bits of carrot confettied Eva, from the crown of her head to her shoulders. I jumped out of my chair and began swatting at her hair. Rico whipped to Eva's side.

The bullfighter hurried over. *"¿Qué pasa, Señorita?"* His eyes flashed sea-foam green and fixed on me.

"It's nothing…it's nothing…uh, *gracias, gracias*, El Victor," I stammered.

Manuel rushed up, mouth wide, forehead rippled. *"¿Qué pasa?"* He reached for a napkin and dabbed at flecks of food entangled in Eva's hair.

"The waitress must've spilled some rice," Rico said. "An accident, nothing more."

"Perhaps, *pero* this *señorita* was 'decorated' as well." El Victor peered at the back of my head.

"*Ay, no, Señor*, clumsiness, I'm sure." Manuel reddened.

"No harm done." Rico smiled. *"Gracias,* Manuel. No problem, right girls?"

Eva doe-eyed her assent. I nodded, which sent more rice flying. I batted my lashes at El Victor, while his eyes flitted about at the stuff.

Manuel nodded, tilted a tiny bow goodbye and hurried away, mumbling under his breath. I watched as he snapped his fingers and several waiters gathered round, whipped their heads in our direction, then back at him. He yanked at his jacket, stiffened and headed for the kitchen. The waiters remained, huddled together, then dispersed.

"There, it's all gone." El Victor flicked the last pea from my hair.

Rico extended his arm and shook the young bullfighter's hand. "I'm Rico de la Lana. *Tantas gracias.*"

"De nada, no problem," the matador said. "José de la Victoria." He bowed.

"And these are my young friends, María Inmaculada and María Evangelina." Rico beamed.

El Victor took my hand in both of his, lifted it and held his eyes steady on mine as he lowered moist lips and warm breath over my wrist. A tingle quivered through me down to my feet, which I pigeon-toed to steady myself in Lola's high heels. My eyes riveted to a spot on the floor when he released his hold on me and turned to Eva.

"That tickles!" I heard Eva giggle-snort. She yanked her hand away from the famous matador.

"Of course, please forgive me, *Señorita*." I looked up to see El Victor blanch and lower his head. "I must get back to my table. *Con permiso*."

"Please join us after dinner for a toast," Rico said.

"I'd be honored, *gracias*." The bullfighter nodded and strode away.

"That was so embarrassing!" I said when he was out of earshot.

"Yeah, how dare that waitress drench me with rice," Eva said.

"Not that. Your laughing at El Victor, that's what," I said.

"I couldn't help it, Inma. Nobody's ever kissed…"

Shhh!" I leaned in with eyes fixed on several waiters who approached brandishing brooms and dustpans. "What's for dessert, Rico?" I ignored the whooshing behind me.

Rico reached for his cognac. "Mango cake. They have the best!"

"Yum!" I said and glanced at Eva.

"All that was on my head?" she wondered aloud and stared at the floor.

"Shall I bring dessert, *Señor*?" one of the waiters asked. Several other waiters quickly swept away the remnants of rice casserole from the floor.

Rico nodded. "And more La Contesa!"

"Inma, have I still got food in my hair?" Eva rattled her head.

"We got it all out," Rico muttered.

"Are you sure?" Eva whined.

"We'll freshen up after dessert," I hissed through clenched teeth.

*   *   *

In the powder room, Eva and I combed out each other's hair.

"I know that jealous waitress deliberately spilled rice on us. I hope Manuel fires her! " Eva said.

"He probably will."

"What nerve! How did she do it, Inma?"

"*Ay*, Eva, I swear, you never notice things."

"I do so. Maybe not like you, Inma, 'the walking telescope.' "

"Anyway, the girl with the rice. I kept looking at all her moles," I confessed.

"And you nag at me for staring!"

"You don't stare, you gawk! Do you want to hear this or not?"

151

"I'm on the edge of my seat." Eva scooted closer to the mirror, applied red lipstick in smooth strokes. "Moles…who notices moles?"

"*Ay, pero* they were everywhere, I'm telling you. You'd have to be blind not to notice. Like dotted-Swiss…*pero* the point is she caught me looking and gave me a frown so ugly I never glanced back at her."

"So that's how she did it!" Eva said.

"Sure, since you never notice stuff and Rico never looks at 'hired help.' "

"What's that supposed to mean, Inma?" Eva turned to look at me.

"*Ay,* never mind! What did you think of El Victor?" I said.

"He's handsome, what else! And he likes you." Eva smiled.

"You really think so?" I fluffed my hair and blinked at my reflection.

"Enjoyed his slobbering your wrist, didn't you?" She laughed.

"You're too much, Eva. Besides, I'm sure he likes you more!"

"You really think so?" she mocked.

I smirked at her in the mirror and laughed. She crossed her eyes and swan-necked her wrist. *"Aja, macho."* She shuffled closer to the mirror. *"Aja."*

My body rocked from laughter and guffaws. Eva's fun ricocheted in recurring squeal-giggle-snorts even after I begged for mercy. "Stop it! *Ay*, my stomach. I'll pee in my pants!" I shoved her.

"He'll never kiss you if you do that!" She sashayed around.

We were still gasping for breath between giggles when several women walked in.

I straightened up and smoothed my dress. *"Vámonos.* We mustn't keep the boys waiting." I signaled to Eva.

Chapter Twelve: Dancing and Sidestepping

As Eva and I started across the dance floor, the orchestra struck up the first number of the evening, a *danzón*, and we were soon engulfed in a sea of satin, sequins and bow ties that churned clockwise, a rhythmic mass of thrusting hips and swinging arms. We bobbed and elbowed our way through the throng. Rico stood and beamed when we emerged at our table.

"El Victor has gone to the bar to celebrate for now, *pero* he has agreed to join us later. This is exciting, *muchachas*. Something you shall remember always." He reached for his drink.

"We owe it all to you," Eva said. "A toast to Rico." She lifted her mineral water and waited for me to do the same. "To our dear friend and distinguished chaperone, Rico. *Muchísimas gracias. Salud.*"

"For putting up with our antics," I said. "*Salud.*" We clinked our glasses together and sipped.

"Look who's here!" Rico said.

I squinted at a group of men approaching and gasped. "Don't look! Don't look! It's the bullfighter who got gored." I whipped my head away.

Eva turned completely around in her chair and narrowed her eyes. "Where? Which one?"

"Never mind! You're impossible."

"You mean that limping skeleton? I didn't recognize him without the bull's horn stuck in his rear end." Eva tossed back her head and giggled.

"The hip, not his *nalga*!" I grabbed my fan, laughed behind it and watched him approach.

He wobbled a bit with each step and nodded a tentative greeting in our direction. Rico chuckled, tipped his head in return.

"Be nice, *muchachas*." Rico smiled and sipped his cognac.

The young matador shuffled to the next table and leaned over to speak to the other bullfighters. Their amusement rumbled our way.

"They're looking over here!" I reported.

Eva's mirth escalated to guffaws that, mercifully, were drowned out by a fresh rendition from the band, an ominous piece entitled "La Noche Negra."

"*¡Ay, Dios Santo!* He's coming over here!" I shrank in my chair.

Eva stifled her giggles with a hand over her mouth at this news. Rico swayed to the music. "*Muchachas, calma.* I'll do the talking. Don't worry."

"Look at him! *Todo chueco*, he's crooked," Eva squeaked. "Look, *prima!*"

"Shush!" I cringed.

"*Buenas tardes, Señor, Señoritas.*" The young man lowered his head, blushed, hesitated.

"*Buenas tardes*," Rico toned, matter-of-fact.

"Permit me to introduce myself." The youth looked a question mark, blinked at us and sighed.

"*¡Cómo no!* You're El Chico. Quite a show today." Rico smiled at him, glanced toward us. "You remember El Chico, *muchachas*."

I bobbed my head behind my fan. Eva covered her mouth and ducked aside to recover something invisible from the floor. The tablecloth trembled beside her.

"I'm Miguel...Miguel del Charco, *su servidor*." He bowed.

"Rico de la Lana, *mucho gusto*." Rico stayed put. "Won't you join us?" Everything on the table jerked an inch closer to Eva as she gripped the tablecloth.

"Eep!" she hiccupped, sat bolt upright, reached for her fan.

"*Gracias, pero* I wish to dance with the young lady." His head twitched in my direction.

I fired a look of panic at Rico.

Eva dove aside again. "Eep...eep!"

"No, I insist." Rico waved his arm at an empty chair. "We're expecting El Victor for a toast. You must stay."

"Uh, may we dance first?" He looked at me.

"You haven't been introduced. Have a seat," Rico said.

"I'm afraid I can't, *Señor*." The young man pointed at his hip.

"*Ay, sí*, of course. What a shame, your...accident." Rico stared boldly. "A dance might be painful as well, *¿no?*"

"I'd be willing to risk it." El Chico thrust back his shoulders.

"Noble of you. Isn't it, *muchachas*?" Rico turned to us.

I nodded. "*Sí, pero* what might it be like for your dance partner?" I said to El Chico. Before he could answer I leaned aside and tugged Eva upright.

"Eep?...Pardon me." She grinned, reached for her drink.

"What do you mean?" El Chico gazed at me.

"She'd have to be brave as well." I jutted out my chin.

"Ahem! Let me introduce you," Rico interrupted and began the formalities.

Just as Eva and I chimed a flat *"mucho gusto"*, El Victor strolled up, champagne bottle in hand, Manuel in tow.

"Hola, Chico. So you've met my friends?" El Victor waved his arm.

El Chico gestured toward me. "I was just trying to convince this young lady to dance with me."

"Hold on, *amigo.* Let's have a drink first!" El Victor boomed.

Within seconds, Manuel squeaked loose the cork until it popped from the bottle. He spun the frothy gush away from us, turned back to pour drinks all around. He set the champagne bottle on the table and smiled a farewell.

"A toast to El Victor!" Rico stood.

The famous matador flicked a hand in the air. "La Noche Negra" met an early dawn, died mid-note. Befuddled dancers bumped against each other, struggled for balance on the dance floor and craned their necks for a better view of the dismayed musicians on stage. The emcee jumped behind the microphone. *"Su atención, por favor...Damas y caballeros*, pour yourselves a drink so we may all join in a toast to our guest of honor, the best matador *en todo el mundo*, El Victor!" At this, El Chico, head hung low, hobbled away without saying a word.

Meanwhile, loud cheers filled the air and filtered through the turmoil as everyone scrambled back to tables, grabbed bottles, readied drinks and called out to waiters, who frenzied back and forth from the bar. When the hall settled into a semblance of anticipation, the emcee again tapped the microphone.

"And to make the toast, I call on a distinguished member of this club, Don Rico de la Lana!" He flung out an arm and dipped into a bow.

Rico beamed, slapped his arm around El Victor's shoulders and raised his champagne, arm straight.

"For bringing great honor and classic grace to our humble bullring this afternoon and to all future successes of the most talented matador ever, we drink to you, *el gran victorioso*, El Victor. *¡Salud!"*

He turned and made a great show of touching glasses with the famous matador. El Victor froze a poster-board smile while several newspaper photographers jockeyed for position around him, their camera bulbs sputtering a blinding blaze around us.

Cries of "*¡Salud!*" collided with loud whistles and tinkling glasses, some of which shattered in the hubbub.

I couldn't see whose wine glass hit mine. I rubbed my eyes. El Victor crooked a finger in the bar's direction. An army of mariachis circled our table. I recognized Rico's stained trousers snugged tight under a violinist's belly. The announcer's voice boomed. "I present to you, all the way from Monterrey, Nuevo Leon, *El Mariachi Ataca La Maraca.*"

"Ta-ta-ra-ta-ta…" A trumpet hammered out an introductory crescendo and the mariachis tightened their circle around us. Other instruments soon clamored along, heightened the musical frenzy and spilled into the fast-paced folkloric dance rhythm. Several mariachis bellowed familiar lyrics that wrapped us tighter in the music's grip. Eva's head swayed from side to side. My feet tapped out the beat under the table.

One of the men wheezed as he sang behind me. I fanned hard at puffs of his garlic breath and managed a grin for the violinist across the table. One musician balanced a bobbing guitar against his belly, tossed back his head, eyes to the heavens and yodeled words of adulation and unrequited love. I squirmed at the sight of his moustache jerking about, a pinnacled toupee in some cosmic tug of war.

El Victor swooped a sombrero from one of the mariachis and placed it on Rico's head. He grabbed another from a musician who offered it at arm's length, chuckling. The famous Spanish matador stomped his heels flamenco-style and held folded hands across his lower back, mimicking Mexican folkloric style. Rico thumped his boots and shuffled, slumped forward, hands clasped behind him, a truer version of the male stance. Both men beamed and laughed as they sashayed around each other.

They soon had an audience whistling, clapping and shouting for more. El Victor raised hands overhead, snapped castanet fingers and whirled about. Women's squeals pierced the air. Men howled *"Ajúa!"* Everyone gathered round to watch as cameras flashed once again.

Eva cupped hands over ears and frowned in my direction. I aimed an eyes-right at Rico, who had assumed the traditional female stance and hopped about, arms in a wingspread, fingers clasping an invisible skirt. El Victor yanked the sombrero from Rico's head, tossed it to the floor and shuffled around it. The cheering around us grew so loud it drowned out the music until the final *"tan-tan."*

"¡Muchachos! Play *'Solamente Una Vez'* for me," El Victor boomed to the mariachis and waved an

arm over us. "I want to dedicate it to my new friends."
His eyes bore into mine. I dizzied as a warm rush of
surprise and panic swept through me. Eva kicked me
under the table and smirked. Rico bowed a marionette's
gracias for the recognition.

Several guitars plucked out the first notes of the
requested number, and El Victor began to sing. The
audience stilled in awe. Sighs and whispers of approval
buzzed in my ears: *"¡Un Agustín Lara!", "¡Gran
talento!", "¡Ay, papacito!"* The famous young matador,
perhaps the best of all time, seemed to focus his
attention only on me. He strolled in my direction and
placed a hand on the back of my chair. I studied a bottle
of liquor on the table and prayed against evil eye from
all the envious stares.

Eva snapped open her fan. I glanced up and
followed her gaze over my shoulder. He was singing to
her! I turned to look at him. El Victor's eyes ping-
ponged from Eva's to mine and back. He turned on his
heel, swung the sombrero high in the air and held the
final notes of the song until his voice cracked. The
mariachis fired a premature *"tan-tan"* as his saving
grace. The matador smiled and bowed from the waist to
his rowdy admirers.

"Gracias, muchachos." He dismissed the
mariachis with a nod, and they promenaded away
performing, wide smiles in place. Loud applause and
cheers continued as some of the audience rushed toward

El Victor, but Rico took him by the arm and whisked him away toward the bar. The crowd dispersed. Some of the girls glared in our direction. I fanned the bad luck away.

"Did you see that?" I hissed to Eva.

"Don't pay attention. They're just jealous, Inma."

"Not that! I mean El Victor. He only pretended his song was for me," I said.

"What do you mean? What are you talking about?" Eva fluffed her hair.

"He kept looking at you!"

"Maybe he did, so what? Are you jealous, Inma?"

"Huh? Me? No, no. It's not that."

"Maybe he likes us both!" Eva said.

"It's the way he looked at you. I know he likes you better," I said.

"Don't be silly, Inma. Who cares anyway? Don't get upset with me."

"You? I'm upset with him," I scoffed.

"*Ay, pues gracias a Dios* for that." Eva shook her head and tossed contagious giggles my way.

We were still laughing when Rico and El Victor returned. The band struck up a melancholy *bolero*. Rico extended a hand to Eva, while El Victor did the same for me. I blushed and glanced at Rico, who nodded approval before I took the matador's hand.

He held my arm aloft until we reached the dance floor, where he launched into a smooth lead and matched precise moves with the marked tempo. I felt myself float across the dance floor, back-and-forth as we danced.

"You dance very well," he commented. Step, step, turn.

"I'm just following your lead, *Señor*." I blushed.

"*Ah, pero*, not everyone follows so well." He grinned. Turn, step, step.

I tried to smile the "go away, closer" look La Cleopatra had taught me. Instead, I noticed his eyes were fixed on my cousin as she and Rico danced by. I cleared my throat. He did not flinch.

He asked, "Tell, me…is Mariá Evangelina your best friend?"

I puffed out a sigh. "No, she is my first cousin, *pero* we are like sisters. We call her Eva, by the way."

"I see. She certainly is beautiful," he said. Step, turn, step.

"Ah, yes," I replied. "EVERYBODY thinks so."

He twirled me about the dance floor. "You are just as beautiful…in a different way."

I missed a step, bumped into him. "*Ay, gracias.*"

"Does it surprise you to hear that I find you just as beautiful?" He beamed. Sidestep, step, step.

"I've been told that MANY times." I rolled my eyes.

He chuckled. "*Pero* you know you truly are." Step, turn, turn.

I shook my head and nearly stumbled. "It's just that I'm told that mostly by Eva's admirers." I looked at him and narrowed my eyes.

He smiled and nodded. "I see." Turn, step, step. "I apologize if I've offended you." He furrowed his brow and waited. Sidestep, sidestep.

"*Ay, no*, you haven't. I'm used to it. It just gets tiresome to constantly hear about my BEAUTIFUL cousin." I rolled my eyes again

"I'm sorry to disappoint you," he said. Step, step, turn.

"No, no. Not at all. " I shook my head. "Like I said, I'm used to it." I managed a sheepish grin.

"Did you enjoy the bullfight?" he asked. Sidestep, step.

"Very much. Did you?"

"*Sí*, I especially enjoyed tossing my cap to you." His eyes searched mine. Sidestep, sidestep.

167

"I thought what bullfighters most like is to wave *adiós* to the bull." I smiled.

"Heh, heh, heh, very good, *Señorita*." His eyes fixed on mine. I looked away.

An orchestral *"tan-tan"* brought the number to a close. El Victor released me and bowed slightly. Rico and Eva emerged from among the dancers who remained abuzz on the floor waiting for the next dance.

"Such talent!" Rico exclaimed. "El Victor makes an art of bullfighting, sings like a professional and provides quite a show on the dance floor! You two did very well! Didn't they, Eva?"

"Beautifully." Eva smirked.

"You see, young lady?" El Victor looked at me, then at Rico. "She argued with me when I told her she followed well."

"I did not!" I shook my head.

"You didn't argue, or you didn't follow well?" Eva tossed her head aside with a laugh. Rico and El Victor joined in.

Their collective amusement rattled me for a moment, but when Eva began snorting loudly between giggles, I smiled and nodded at them. Eva grew hysterical with laughter.

"Calm down, *muchacha*." Rico chuckled at her. "She needs to drink some water," he said as he led her away.

El Victor and I followed them to the table. I watched as the famous matador spoke to Rico, who smiled broadly and nodded.

Once Eva quit giggling, I heard El Victor ask her, "May I have the next dance?"

Eva glanced at Rico for his approval and blushed. She smiled at El Victor, who extended his hand to her. They proceeded to the dance floor.

"Would you like to dance, Inma?" Rico asked.

"I think I'd rather sit this one out if it's all right with you," I said.

"What's happened?" He frowned.

"The usual. El Victor went on and on about Eva while we danced," I scoffed.

"All the more reason to dance with me. Don't let him see you are disappointed. Come now, let's dance." He held out his hand.

As we began to dance I realized that Rico had been wise to coax me onto the dance floor. The music was a lively rumba and soon I was enjoying myself. Everyone danced in a circle. When I spied Eva and El Victor across the dance floor, she looked at me and crossed her eyes. Soon she and I were both giggling. El Victor didn't seem to notice or was too polite to make anything of it, but Rico frowned at me.

"What are you and Eva up to? El Victor is a world famous matador. You two should be honored to dance with him. This is something you will always remember."

"I liked the dance," I responded. "It was the conversation that disappointed me." Turn, step, turn.

"Don't be silly, Inma." Rico shook his head.

"It's just that I didn't expect a world famous matador to be like ALL the others."

"We've been through this before, Inma," Rico said. Step, step, turn.

"That's what I mean. *Pero* you're right. Let's just dance!" I insisted.

When the music stopped, we returned to the table. Rico and El Victor pulled out chairs so that Eva and I could be seated, then they headed to the bar talking boisterously. As soon as they stepped away, I turned to Eva and asked, "Well, how was it? Did you enjoy being in the limelight with the famous El Victor?"

Eva giggled. "The same old thing. He went on about how he found me beautiful. Then he said it is a shame he is leaving tomorrow. He truly wishes he could see me again. Blah, blah, blah." She rolled her eyes.

"Maybe he'll give up the rest of his tour for you!" I smiled.

"You are too funny, Inma!" She grinned. "What did you think of your dance with him?"

"*Pues*, it was also all about your beauty. Then, of course, he offered the usual consolation all your admirers give when they realize I might be tired of hearing about *you*—that he found *me* just as beautiful in a different way. The USUAL! Blah, Blah, blah."

"*Ay*, Inma, I'm sorry he bored you. *Pero* he did say he first noticed us because of the flowers in our hair, like the girls back home in Spain. Can you imagine?"

I laughed. "And what did you say to that?"

"A smile and nod was all I could muster. I had to hold back a giggle," Eva replied. "Anyway, I think you are more beautiful than I am, Inma. And who cares? You carry on conversations while I usually smile and say nothing. We're too young to pay attention to any flattery if you ask me."

"You're right, Eva. Who cares?" Suddenly I saw Rico and El Victor returning, drinks in hand. "Shh, shh, here they come!" I whispered. Eva and I smiled as they took their seats at the table.

Rico beamed. "*Muchachas*, El Victor has been telling me about himself. Now I see why he is so talented, not only in the bullring, but also on the dance floor. Tell the girls about your younger days," he insisted.

"*Pues*," El Victor said, "I sang and danced to earn a living until I established myself as a bullfighter. I performed in cafés next to bullrings all over Spain. Waited tables, shined shoes, whatever I could. It took years, so I got lots of practice." He shrugged.

"You see, *muchachas*, El Victor developed many talents!" Rico boomed and waved an arm in the air.

El Victor continued. "Did you see those boys jump into the arena this afternoon, eager for a chance at the bull?" Eva and I nodded. "That's how I got started. Before that, I perfected my cape-work with a towel while my brother played the bull." He held straightened forefingers, one on either side of his head and smiled.

I giggled. "*Very scary.*"

"Heh, heh, you don't know my brother!"

Chapter Thirteen: Afternoon Social—Interrupted!

Violins swirled into a dreamy waltz. Couples on the dance floor stepped toward each other again.

"Shall we dance?" El Victor turned to Eva. She glanced at Rico, who nodded. El Victor pulled out her chair and led her to the dance floor.

"Surely we'll all get the evil eye, Rico," I said, "especially Eva."

Rico tossed back his head and laughed loudly. "*¡Ah, qué muchacha!* Always the worrier."

When the music stopped, El Victor and Eva emerged from the thicket of dancers.

"Enjoying yourselves?" Rico beamed.

"Most definitely." El Victor glanced at Eva. She nodded demurely.

"You danced very well together," Rico observed. I bobbed my head.

Suddenly Eva turned to me and hissed, "Look, who's here!" El Victor furrowed his brows. "It's our hairdresser," Eva whispered to the matador.

La Cleopatra floated up, Elegancia at her side. Their gowns looked like tubes of colorful Christmas wrapping paper, one scarlet, the other emerald green, wrapped tightly about their slender figures.

"*Hola, muchachas, Señores*," said La Cleopatra, her voice a playful growl. She nodded and batted her lashes. Elegancia grinned, her head low, eyes on El Victor.

"*Hola*," Eva and I chimed.

"*Buenas tardes,* my beauties!" Rico's voice dripped honey. "Did you enjoy the bullfight?" His eyes darted toward El Victor.

"*Ay, sí*, Rico, it was fantastic!" La Cleopatra's penciled eyebrows stood high above glittered eyelids. "*Tantas gracias.* And the seats were perfect, as usual. We saw every move the matadors made." Her cat eyes crawled up and down El Victor.

"Then you've seen this young fellow?" Rico nodded at the matador, who stepped forward. "Let me introduce to you," Rico looked at El Victor, "our dear friend Cleonicia Flores."

175

"*Mucho gusto*, José de la Victoria." He reached for La Cleopatra's already-extended arm, bowed his head and brushed his lips across her hand. La Cleopatra shimmied delight.

"Introduce me!" Elegancia pinched Eva's elbow. Eva turned to conduct the formalities but stopped when El Victor approached Elegancia with a smile and introduced himself. She giggled as he kissed her hand and grabbed at his shoulder to steady herself when her knees buckled.

"And now, I must ask that you pardon me," El Victor said. "I have to get back to my friends or they will never forgive me. *Muchas gracias* for allowing me the pleasure of your company this evening." He smiled at us and walked away.

"Isn't he handsome?" Rico said.

"*Ay, muy, muy.*" La Cleopatra nodded then turned to me. "What happened to your hair? Rico, I hope you don't think *that* is what you paid for." Red fingernail polish flashed in my face as she flapped her hand at my head.

"*Ay, por favor*," I pleaded. "We had to comb it out. The dust stuck to all that hairspray."

"Where's your hat?" she asked, as if I'd just yanked it off.

"We wore flowers."

"*Pues*, that's the problem. What a shame. I hope you saw their hair before the dust, Rico." La Cleopatra studied his face.

"Lovely!" He smiled and nodded.

"When are you coming by to see me?" La Cleopatra took Rico's arm.

"Let's dance, shall we?" he responded. She faced him and dipped into a swing of her hips. He chuckled and contorted his version.

"Let's get out of here!" I laughed and yanked Elegancia out of their way.

"Saved by the music!" Eva said as we reached the table.

"Have a seat, Elegancia." I waved an arm toward an empty chair.

"Can't." She shook her head. "I promised the next dance to one of the matadors." She spun a search on tiptoes.

"Which one? Which one?" I asked.

"The one who got hurt. Did you see? Poor thing. The fortune teller was right. Something bad did happen today."

"You think that was it?" Eva said.

"What else?" said Elegancia.

"I don't know. He wasn't hurt that badly." I shrugged.

"*Ay*, here he comes! Here he comes! He's found me even in this crowd. How romantic!" Elegancia sighed.

I looked up to see the maimed matador hobble toward us. "Him?" I asked.

"*Ay, sí*, isn't he handsome?"

Before I could say I didn't think so, he came within earshot.

"Vamos." He reached for Elegancia's hand, smirked at me.

On the dance floor, she stood stiff and held both his hands while he stirred his hips about. I searched the dance floor for Rico and La Cleopatra, but it seemed as if everyone in the place was dancing, the crowd was so thick. Suddenly, a ripple of dancers struggled aside and opened a path across the ballroom. Screams pierced the air. The music came to a dead stop. Dancers bumped into each other. People scratched and squealed to get away from the commotion. Chairs upended. One woman slipped to the floor. Several men stepped around her while her husband struggled to rescue her.

"SHE'S GOT A KNIFE!" A hysterical cry rang loud. One of the waitresses scrambled through the room toward a pair of dancers. She yelled to warn them. "She's going to kill El Victor!"

Eva and I watched as a wild-eyed woman, long wavy hair flying behind her, a butcher knife clutched high over her head, ran after El Victor. People shrieked and scrambled about. A young woman fainted and two men quickly dragged her from the dance floor.

As the hysterical woman whipped the knife at El Victor, she let out a feral scream, *"¡COBARDE!...*Turn and face me, you coward!"

I stared as the world's most famous matador ran for his life, dodging the shiny blade. He whirled about on his heel, bobbed and threaded through the crowd. He stumbled away from the dance floor toward the tables. More screams, squeals and shoves as everyone scattered, spilling chairs, tables and each other.

Eva and I scrambled from the table. We elbowed our way toward the bandstand, where we climbed onstage to search for Rico and La Cleopatra. I spied them in the distance and flailed my arms about. Rico caught sight of me, waved and pointed to the kitchen as he and La Cleopatra trailed one of the waitresses.

Eva and I hurried from the stage, hunched forward, nuzzled against a large man's back as he lumbered toward the casino entrance. Every few steps, I peeked around him. I saw Rico and La Cleopatra struggle against the flow of others who streamed toward the exits.

"Come this way!" Rico called as we approached. Eva and I traipsed after them into the kitchen. I recognized the waitress who had come to our rescue. She was the one who had spilled rice on us earlier. She blinked at me and nodded, her face somber.

"*Vamos.*" She led us to the back door.

Suddenly, I remembered our evening bags—the ones we'd borrowed from Lola—and groaned. "Our purses, Rico!"

"Your purses? What do you mean, Inma? Where did you leave them?" He kept one hand on my shoulder and continued to nudge me along.

"We left them on the table. The evening bags!" I puffed at Eva's back. She kept moving.

"I'll have her fetch them." Rico lifted his chin toward the waitress.

"And our fans," I whined.

The waitress pushed open the back door, her eyes wide. As we hurried out, Rico turned to her.

"Get the girls' things from our table and give them to Manuel. I'll send someone to collect them tomorrow. Understand, *muchacha?*"

"*O, sí...sí Señor.* I understand." She nodded and narrowed her eyes.

"We'll never see those bags again," Eva whispered to me and giggled.

"You won't find it so humorous when Lola finds out," I said.

"Hush, *muchachas.*" Rico put an arm around each of us as we hurried away.

Chapter Fourteen: "That Evil Fortune Teller"

The next morning before dawn, I woke to loud knocking coming from the front door. *"¡Mamá!"* I called out and headed toward the noise.

"¿Qué pasa?" Mamá hurried from the kitchen, still wearing an apron. She followed me into the store and stood beside me as I swung open the narrow doors. Doña Inez waved and smiled broadly.

"Buenos días," she sang. "How are you? It's a lovely morning isn't it?"

"Pues, it's still dark," I said. "What is it?" Mamá poked me and I cleared my throat. "I mean, what can we do for you, Doña Inez?"

"I need more sugar," she said. "This time it's for my daughter Elegancia. You know, I hadn't seen her in months... months! *Pero,* I went to look for her." The old woman beamed. "To see if she knew where her father was. He didn't come home last night."

"¿Pero cómo? How? Where is he? Have you found him?" Mamá said.

"*Ah, no.* Nor do I care to. He's run off with that conniving fortune teller!"

"*¡Dios mío!* How can that be?" Mamá gasped. "Are you sure?"

"*Ay, sí*, that witch was sure to leave me a note I could read this time. 'Your husband loves me. We are going away', she writes. 'Don't bother to look for us.' Can you believe the nerve of that woman?" Doña Inez blinked, waited. Mamá and I looked at each other.

"*Pues*, I'm...I'm shocked, Doña." Mamá spoke first. "Aren't you?...I mean, are you all right?"

"I'm fine! Only, Elegancia got the fright. She has a bad case of *susto*. *Pobrecita*. It's not that she'll miss her father. She's upset about all the gossip she'll hear at the beauty salon where she works. That's what those women do all day, you know. Get pampered and air out everyone's dirty laundry. Says she'll die of humiliation.

"This must be what the fortune teller meant about something awful happening," I murmured.

"Awful? *Ay, no, mija.* She'll get hers. You'll see. That husband of mine is no prize. Last night, I slept better than I have in years! Now SHE'LL have to listen to his snoring. She'll regret this, all right. What a relief for me. No more, 'Make my coffee...What's for

184

dinner?…Rub my feet.' His smelly feet are gone. The joke's on her." The old woman cackled. "Don't you see?"

Mamá and I bobbed our heads.

"*Bueno, pues*, I'll get your sugar. How much would you like?" Mamá said.

"Just a cupful for now." She handed Mamá a coin. "I need to keep some of the money for more holy candles." She grinned at me.

"So they helped," I said.

"*Ay, sí.* You gave me good advice. I followed your instructions and everything worked out. The candles kept evil away, all right. I'll burn one every day from now on to make sure those two never come back." She grinned. *"Gracias, mija."*

Mamá handed her a small paper cone that held the sugar.

Doña Inez wrapped her wrinkled brown hands around the treasured cure for fright and nodded, eyes glazed. *"Que Dios las bendiga.* Bless you, bless you both!...*Bueno*, I must get back to my daughter. Then I'm

185

off to get more candles. *Con permiso*." She glowed merry mischief.

"*Vaya con Dios,* Doña," Mamá said.

The old woman hobbled to the door and turned around. "I just remembered. Elegancia said one of the matadors got stabbed by his jealous wife at the casino last night. You were there, weren't you?" She gazed at me.

I looked at Mamá and hesitated. "*Sí, pero* we left as soon as that woman came after him. I didn't know he'd been hurt."

"Why didn't you tell me about this, Inma?" Mamá turned to me.

"I didn't want to worry you," I said.

"The matador wasn't hurt badly. And the woman was taken to jail," Doña Inez said. "Funny, isn't it…he outran a bull all afternoon *pero* he got caught by his wife. He probably had too much tequila."

"He's okay, then?" I asked.

"That's the gossip according to a matador who escorted Elegancia and La Cleopatra home. Anyway, I guess something terrible did happen after all, only not to me!" Doña Inez grinned.

"*Bueno, gracias,* Doña," Mamá said.

"*De nada.*" The old woman nodded and left.

Mamá studied my face. "Maybe I should give you some sugar."

"I'm fine, *pero* I'm sure a piece of candy would make me feel even better."

Mamá smiled, opened a glass jar on the counter and handed me a lollipop. "I'm just relieved you didn't witness something so violent."

"Me too."

"*Por favor*, Inma, no more advice for Doña Inez about candles or casting spells."

"*Pero*, everything turned out okay. She's happy!" I jutted my chin.

"*Sí, pero* when others find out about this, you'll have a line of people seeking your help." She smirked.

"You're right! I could charge each one a *peso* and make lots of money."

Mamá shook her head. "No more spells."

"Of course not, Mamá."

Chapter Fifteen: Cinderellas No More

"Batter up!" My brother Refugio called from the middle of the dusty road later that afternoon. Several of the neighborhood kids had joined us for a baseball game.

Eva and I sat on the stoop in front of Mamá's store. The magic of the night before was over, yet it was all we could think of. Instead of fancy dresses and flowers in our hair, we wore dusty trousers and baseball caps borrowed from our brothers.

"I still can't believe it," Eva said. "El Victor, married. What a CHEAT!"

"Guess he paid for that," I said.

"Inma, are you playing or not? You're up!" My brother put hands to hips.

"Coming!" I waved and hurried to the makeshift home plate, a ragged burlap sack stuffed with dirt and pebbles. I signaled an okay for him to fire the first pitch. The ball whirled toward me. I swung the stick we used as a bat, sent the ball flying and scrambled to first base, a scrawny mesquite.

"Come on, Eva! Hit a good one. Bring me in!" I yelled to my cousin.

"One homerun, coming up." Eva smiled and sauntered toward the plate.

"We'll see about that!" my brother yelled.

Eva squinted in the afternoon sun and took a wild swing at the first pitch.

"Strike one!" someone called. "Hey, *muchacho*, loosen up those knees."

All of us turned to look at the stranger. It took me a few seconds to recognize him in street clothes. El Victor stood, his bandaged arm in a sling, pressing a bouquet of roses against his chest.

"Go ahead, pitch! Don't hold up the game on my account." He nodded at my brother.

"You're the matador! Hey, look who's here!" Refugio said to the other kids. "Aren't you El Victor? I recognize you from the posters."

"*Pues, sí*, I am." The matador lowered his head, shifted his feet in the dirt then looked at my brother.

"*Oye, muchacho*, maybe you can help me. I'm looking for a young lady named Eva."

"Eva? What do you want with her? You brought her those flowers?" Refugio scoffed.

"*Pues, sí*, they're for her. I need to see her...uh, to apologize for what happened last night."

"*Ah, sí*, you mean that scandal at the casino. Your jealous wife almost killed you." My brother scowled at the world famous matador.

"She's not my wife. Just a woman I met on tour. I want to clear up the gossip."

"Go ahead, *Señor*. There's Eva." Refugio leaned his head toward home plate. Eva blinked at El Victor from under her dusty cap, a crooked smile across her smudged face.

El Victor's eyes widened. "Where? Where is she?"

"Eva! Wave to the nice bullfighter, would you?" Refugio looked at Eva.

Eva looked at me and giggled. I laughed as she cupped her fingers and motioned them up and down at the famous matador.

El Victor's eyebrows arched high. "Why is that boy waving? *¿Qué pasa?* Where's Eva?"

Some of the boys snickered.

"Get over here, *muchachas*!" My brother flapped an arm in the air and approached El Victor.

Eva and I giggled as we walked toward them. Since each of us wore boy's trousers and suspenders, El Victor had assumed we were boys. As we neared the matador, I yanked off my cap, then Eva's. We let down our hair and shook the dust from our caps.

El Victor's flowers plopped to the ground. He squirmed. "*Dios mío*, you're just kids. *¡Niñas!* How old are you?" He gazed at Eva and me.

"We're fourteen if you must know. What do you think about that?" I scoffed. Eva stifled a giggle.

"*Pero* last night you looked so...so...I mean, I thought..."

"That you'd made a new conquest?" Refugio taunted the matador. "*Pues*, you were wrong. See? They're just two kids who like to play dress up. Right, *muchachas*?" He glared at us. Eva and I shrugged.

"I...uh, I apologize. I assure you, I had no idea," El Victor said. "I just wanted to explain."

"No need!" Refugio waved his arms as if to shoo away the famous man. "And in the future I suggest you stick to chasing bulls. It's safer!"

"Pfft!" I unleashed a fit of giggles. The kids around us roared with laughter. El Victor's face strained as if he'd swallowed a razor blade. Amid our howls of laughter, he turned on his heel and hurried away. Several neighbors appeared at their doors.

"*Damas y caballeros*, there goes the great El Victor!" my brother yelled.

The famous man broke into a full sprint.

"See what you girls have done!" Refugio turned to us, hands on hips. "I hope you enjoyed yourselves."

"We didn't do anything!" I said.

"You fooled him with your makeup and fancy clothes. You know you're not supposed to dance with strangers. Besides, he's too old!"

"We did *not* lead him on! Rico said it was okay for us to dance with him. Anyhow, we can't help it if we look sophisticated when we dress up." I turned and looked at Eva.

"It's just for fun." She smiled and nodded.

"That kind of fun can get you killed," Refugio said. "You shouldn't play games with the opposite sex like that."

"You hush! We did no such thing!" I shook my head at the neighborhood boys who'd gathered around us. "Come on, Eva. Let's get out of here!"

"Just wait! I'm telling Mamá!" my brother roared after us. "You'll see. From now on I'll be your only chaperone. Enough with that dandy Rico pal of yours!"

"*Ay, no, por favor*. Don't tell Mamá about this," I pleaded.

"You can't stop me! Besides, everyone in town knows you two danced the night away with that

194

bullfighter. I heard you had to sneak out the kitchen door. You should be ashamed. Both of you. *¡Sin vergüenzas!"*

"*Pues*, we're not!" I jutted my chin at him. "Eva, hurry. We're leaving!" I tossed my head. Eva chuckled and performed a parade wave for everyone.

"What about the game?" Refugio yelled. The other boys groaned.

"You just said we shouldn't play games with the opposite sex! *Adiós, muchachos.*" I tugged at Eva and frowned at my brother and his friends.

"Ha! Looks like more trouble for you." Refugio pointed. "Here comes Lola, and she looks good and angry."

Eva's sister raised puffs of orange dust as she stomped toward us, her fist in the air. Eva and I turned away.

"Come back here right now!" she yelled.

"What's all the commotion?" Mamá called from the stoop. Eva and I froze under her watchful gaze.

Lola stood solemn, an emcee making a public announcement. "Rico's chauffeur came to the house and said the evening purses these two 'Cinderellas' borrowed from me are gone. STOLEN! They left them behind when they ran away from that madwoman with the knife!"

"Did that woman chase you?" Mamá's eyes searched mine.

"No, no!" I shuddered. "I swear she did not!"

"*Tía*, Eva and Inma were with that El Victor character all night!" Lola yelled.

"They are the ones who made that *loca* jealous!" my brother exclaimed.

"*Pero*, Rico was with us the whole time." Eva shook her head.

"Not while you were dancing with the matador!" Lola nodded at Mamá, folded arms across her chest and tapped her foot in the dust.

"You danced with El Victor?" Mamá's eyes rounded.

"We both did," I said and glanced at Eva.

196

Mamá shook her head. "That's the last social you'll attend for a long time."

"*Pero* Rico was with us!" I whined.

"I'll speak to him," Mamá said.

"Let me keep an eye on them from now on." Refugio puffed out his chest.

Mamá narrowed her eyes at my brother. "We'll talk about this later, *hijo*. Meanwhile, you two will pay Lola for those evening bags." She looked at Eva and me.

"We'll get them back!" I said.

"Oh, yeah? How?" Lola snarled.

"Hey, get out of here, you silly girls! We're trying to play ball," Refugio yelled.

Lola turned on her heel. "I'm telling on you, Eva," she called over her shoulder. "First, you dance with a matador twice your age and now this!"

"You better go after her." I shrugged at Eva. "Remember, you've got the goods on her," I whispered as she hurried after her sister.

"Lola, wait! You're forgetting something!" Eva called.

I looked at Mamá and said, "You know what? The fortune teller was right after all. Something awful did happen last night, only it happened to Eva and me instead of Doña Inez." I sighed.

"*Ay, hija,* you have so much to learn," Mamá said. "Don't drown in a cup of water."

"You mean you're not angry?"

"No. That never helps anything, does it?"

"Of course not." I smiled.

"Aren't you going to pick up those poor roses?" Mamá looked behind me as I approached the store.

I turned and blinked at the bouquet in the dust, the only remnant of our adventure with El Victor. I stole toward them, bent my knees and plucked them from the ground. I dusted and sniffed at the flowers as I entered the house. I held them out to Mamá. She grinned and shook her head.

"He brought those for you or for Eva?"

"He liked both of us, Mamá. Truly! He danced with me first."

"Something you'll remember always, *mija*."

"Just think, Mamá, the famous El Victor brought these for Eva and me." I cradled the flowers in my arms. "He chose these roses just like he picked out Eva and me in all that crowd. He tossed us his cap at the bullfight you know."

"Of course I know. It's the talk of the town this morning."

"It is? Who told you?"

"*Ay, mija*, I had more customers this morning than I usually have in an entire week!" Mamá shook her head. "They all want to know which of you the cap was meant for."

"I think he aimed for both of us, really...Okay, maybe he preferred Eva to me, *pero* I know he liked me, too!"

"I'm sure he did, *mija*. We have a lot of things to talk about."

"You knew we danced with him, didn't you?"

She nodded. "You broke one of our rules, *hija*."

"*Pero*, only because it was El Victor! Just think."

"A LOT to talk about." Mamá gazed at me.

"You already said that."

"It's more important than ever, *mija*. One of the customers said everyone's calling you and Eva the 'it' girls of La Sembradora, *las meras meras de* La Sembradora."

"Us? They called us *las meras meras?* The 'it' girls?"

Mamá shrugged. "At least for now, *mija*."

"The 'it' girls. I like the way that sounds."

"Just don't forget you're still girls."

"Sure, *pero*, we're the 'it' girls!" I giggled.

"Plenty of time for all that. Right now, I want you to make *flan* pudding for our dessert."

"*Ay, no, por favor.* You know I always scorch it!"

"You need practice. Be patient. Remember the old saying, 'With patience you can save the nation.' "

"What does that have to do with pudding?" I groaned and followed Mamá into the kitchen. I put the roses in a vase and set them in the middle of the table. As I gathered ingredients for the dessert, I stared at the flowers. Eva wouldn't care if I kept them, I was sure. I sighed then announced to my mother, "I'll share them with Eva, of course!"

"That's my girl," Mamá said.

"Your 'it' girl!" I laughed.

Made in the USA
San Bernardino, CA
18 March 2015